PAULA DANZIGER

The Pistachio Prescription

Penguin Putnam Books
for Young Readers

To Carolyn and Sam Danziger
    for the birth and for their best
To Sam Slipp
    for the understanding

My thanks to Barbara Shimshak Birnbaum,
Gail Feinbloom, Susan Haven,
and Vicki Larsen.

Library of Congress Cataloging-in-Publication Data
Danziger, Paula.
The pistachio prescription.
SUMMARY: A high school "freshperson" attempts to
rise above such inconveniences of life as her older sister,
parents, and school. [1. Family life—Fiction.
2. School stories.] I. Title. PZ7.D2394Pi [Fic] 77-86330
ISBN 0-698-11690-9
10 9 8 7 6 5 4

"In the midst of winter, I finally learned
that there was in me an invincible summer."
—Albert Camus

Chapter 1

Pistachio nuts, the red ones, cure any problem. When I'm upset or nervous, or have a cold or something, I always eat them. My best friend, Vicki, says that's the silliest thing she's ever heard, that there's no medical evidence to prove it's true. She says it's jelly beans that work, that nine out of ten doctors recommend them for patients who have hypochondria. But since I know all my illnesses are real, pistachios are the answer.

I try to keep a bag of them stashed away for breakdown situations. They've got to be hidden because my mother disapproves. "Cassie, red fingers just aren't chic," she says. When I'm out, she sneaks into my room and searches it. I'm the only person I know who gets busted for possession of pistachio nuts. It makes me sick, but she says if I don't like it, I can always move out. There's got to be a hotel somewhere that takes thirteen-year-old kids and doesn't cost more than one dollar a week.

My mother sticks her newly permanented red head into my room. "Cassie, be downstairs in half an hour for breakfast. I want to leave here by nine." She gives her hair a toss as she goes out.

Maybe I should be happy I'm going on a shopping spree for clothes to start the school year. But I hate to shop with her. She nags and doesn't let me pick out the stuff I like the best. She spends a mint, and then my father throws a fit when the bills come in. It's awful—ruins it for me every time. I try to tell her to spend less, but she never listens. She says, "Your grandfather left your father a lot of real estate holdings. He's gotten a lot more since he took over. He'll never hurt for money. So why should we?"

I locate the pistachios, taped to the inside of a frisbee on the top shelf of my closet. I get dressed quickly, shelling the nuts as I put my clothes on. I put the shells into an empty soda can and then stuff paper inside so there's no rattle in case my mother shakes it.

Dressed in record time. I can relax for a few minutes. Going back to bed would be great, but I've already made it, and my mother would yell if she saw me on it. I don't see any reason to make the bed since I'm only going to mess it up again at night. Anyway, she's the one who wanted the canopied bed with all the frilly junk that goes with it. I wanted the bed that's shaped like a giant sneaker. You don't even need a bedspread. You just lace it up. It was the best bed that I saw at Bloomingdale's. "Not stylish enough," she said. So now I've got a room that doesn't even feel like me, not the way I want to feel when I come in to escape from the rest of the world.

I just don't fit in with the rest of my family. I'm sure I'm adopted, that I'm a Martian they found in the backyard and took in for the tax deduction. No one else in the family looks like me. Two have curly red hair and green eyes, my mother and Andrew. My father and Stephie have blond hair and blue eyes. I've got brown hair and brown eyes. The only one I resemble is Mutant, my brother's pet gerbil.

Everyone else has normal names—Andrew, Anne, Andrew, Jr., and Stephanie. I got named Cassandra. Just my luck that my mother was taking a course in Greek mythology right before I was born. (So they say, but I bet they're just trying to make me think I'm not adopted.) Every year, some teacher tells me how it was Cassandra's curse to speak the truth and be thought insane. If that happens one more time, I'm going to scream. Sometimes I'm afraid I'll end up like that other Cassandra. Maybe they make straitjackets in prewashed denim.

We have a plaque in the kitchen that says "Bless Our Happy Home." Andrew gave it to my parents on their last anniversary. He keeps hoping they'll take the hint.

My parents are difficult. That's what they're always saying about me, but they're impossible. Sometimes they are wonderful, sometimes terrible, and I never know which one it's going to be. They hardly ever act the same way at the same time.

Andrew's my favorite, everyone's favorite, as a matter of fact. He's the only thing we all agree on. He collects animals. So far, he's got Mutant; Snurful, the sheepdog; Adam, the garter snake; Tarzan and Jane, the flying squirrels; and the parakeet, Fido. He's the only seven year old I know who wants to be a zoo keeper when he grows up.

As for Stephanie, there aren't enough bad words in the English language to describe her fully. We hardly speak to each other. That's because when she was fourteen and I was ten, I told her new boyfriend she'd stuffed her bra with practically a whole box of Kleenex. Three years is a long time to hold a grudge, especially since she doesn't even wear a bra anymore.

When we're all together, none of us get along. Separately, sometimes, some of us get along, but it's never wonderful.

To top it all off, I've got asthma. Half the time I walk around sounding like a whistling tea pot, and the other half, I turn blue in the face.

I just don't feel as if I really belong in this family. Except for Andrew, no one tries to know who I really am, how I feel about things. If I'm not adopted (and I'd like that, because then I'd know I was really wanted), then I bet some nurse must have gotten the babies mixed up, and I actually belong with another family. Somewhere in the world, I bet, there's a curly-haired blond or redhead with a family who all have straight brown hair and brown eyes, and that person doesn't feel she belongs either.

Halfway through the package of pistachios, I wet my finger and stick it in the salty part. There's a knock on the door.

"Just a minute," I yell.

She walks right in. "Oh, Cassie, not again."

"Hi, Mom." I lick the salt off my fingers. "Want some?"

"At this hour? No thank you. Look at your fingers. You look like an ax murderer."

"Like Lizzie Borden?" I ask, thinking of the woman accused of chopping up her parents.

"You really think you're funny, don't you? I only hope that when you have children, they treat you the same way you treat me."

The asthma's starting. It feels as if water is filling up my lungs and I'm going to drown. Opening my mouth to say something, I start to wheeze. I panic when that starts. That makes it worse, even harder to breathe, but I don't think I can control it. I put my head down to my knees. The pistachios spill on the pink carpet, but I don't even care. I feel as if I've got to fight to get even a little air inside of me.

My mother puts her hand on my head and says, "Cassie, honey, try to relax. After all, we're going to have a wonderful day. You're very lucky. What if you had to wear all of Stephie's hand-me-downs?"

Sure. Stephie's five two, got a bust and hips, and

takes great care of her clothes. There's never anything to hand down that would fit me, since I'm five six, still growing, have no bust worth mentioning, and seem to have misplaced my waist. If I wore her clothes, I'd be arrested for indecent exposure—if I had anything indecent to expose.

I keep gulping for air.

My mother brings over my inhaler.

I use it.

It starts to take effect. Slowly.

She hands me my pills.

I take one.

It's getting a little easier to breathe.

Not good but better.

I take a real deep breath.

It gets sort of caught in the middle.

I go back to the shorter breaths until I'm more in control.

"Darling, do you feel better?" My mother is speaking very softly.

I nod.

"I just want to do something nice with you," she says. "Think of all the poor children who would love to have a mother who could take them to Bloomingdale's."

She should take one of them. Maybe they have fathers who wouldn't scream when the bills come in. If they're poor though, probably not. It's really dumb, that statement, kind of like having to finish your broccoli because of all the starving children in the world. Whenever she mentions that, I want to throw my portion in a mailbox. Let them have it. They can send me their pistachio nuts in return.

"Come on, Cassie, it'll be fun. Two girls on the town."

Two girls. Vomit. She must be kidding. She's almost thirty-seven. Always talking about how young she is to have a seventeen-year-old daughter. Retch.

She continues, "I get so scared when this happens. You know the doctor says you've got to learn to stay calm. That most of this is psychological. You can control the part that's not allergy-related, honey. Just learn to take it easy."

Easy for her. Not easy for me.

I try. "Give me a few minutes alone. I'll be downstairs in a little while."

She gets up, looks at me, and says, "When I was your age, I would have loved it if my mother was able to take me shopping. I'm just trying to please you."

Sad. That's how she always gets when she talks about her mother. It makes me sad, too, that she had multiple sclerosis, and that I never got a chance to know her, and that my mother had to spend years taking care of her. But it's not my fault.

"Mom, we'll have fun." I can feel the medicine working.

She smiles, "Good. I'll see you downstairs in a few minutes."

As she leaves, I look down at the carpet. Now the leftover nuts have pink lint on them. I pick them up and hide them in the middle of a dried-flower arrangement.

I sit back down on my bed and think about how parents change when kids get older. Maybe it's something chemical.

By the time I get downstairs, Andrew and Stephanie are almost done eating.

"Hi," I say, sitting down.

Andrew grins. "Hi, Cassie."

Stephanie, as usual, acts as if I don't exist.

"Where's Dad?" I want to know.

My mother makes a face. "At the golf course, where else?"

Stephanie says, "Mom, where are the keys to your car? Greg's coming over to give me another lesson before I take the test in it."

"What do you mean, the keys? Cassie and I are taking the car to the station." My mother shakes her head.

Stephie screams, "Dad promised. The test's next week. He said I could take your car today since it's the one I'll be using."

"Your father's got no right to promise the use of my car when he takes his to the club. Anyway, you've got to watch Andrew. I can't leave him alone. You can charm your way with your father, but not with me."

"I don't care. He said I could have the car. You're just jealous that I can talk to Dad." Stephie makes a face.

I look at Andrew. He's pretending to eat his breakfast—scrambled eggs with grape jelly and catsup. That's all he ever eats in the morning. For three years now, it's been a ritual.

"Don't you ever talk to me like that!" my mother yells.

Stephie's sitting down, whimpering. The tears roll out of her blue eyes as if they'll never stop. She wants to be an actress someday.

I stare at Andrew. There's a glob of catsup on his nose. It almost matches his hair. I reach over and wipe it off.

"Can't we get a baby-sitter for him?" I ask.

"Why don't you mind your own business, Giraffe," Stephie yells.

That does it. The tears start. Only I don't fake them.

"Now you've made your sister cry. What kind of animal are you? You know how sickly she is," my mother yells.

"She really is sick . . . crazy sick . . . I hate you, all of you! Cassie just coughs or makes those obscene noises, and she gets whatever she wants. I hate you!" She slams out of the room.

My mother comes over and puts her arm around my shoulder. "Cassie, don't worry. You'll probably stop growing someday. Anyway, you've got some wonderful qualities."

I'm glad I took my medicine. I think I may survive this. It'll be close but not fatal.

As she leaves the room, Andrew whispers, "Cassie, you're nicer than either of them. Don't cry. I'll marry you when I get old enough."

Now he's got catsup and grape jelly on his nose. He pats me on the arm.

I smile at him. We sit there without saying anything.

My mother comes in, all smiles. "All settled. Mrs. Brandon will be glad to take Andrew; she says John is looking forward to it."

Andrew crosses his eyes. John still wets his bed. Andrew says it's hard being friends with someone whose room smells like kitty litter.

"And I've got the other problem figured out. Greg's on his way over. He can go to the station with us so that when I leave, there'll still be a licensed driver with Stephie. Then when they get done, they can return the car to the station and leave it there. Your father can follow and pick them up when he gets back." She smiles and seems real proud of herself.

As usual, everything works out for Stephie.

"I'm going in to talk to your sister. Honestly, I don't know what this family would do without me."

In a few minutes, they return. With them is Greg, who's even more gorgeous than they are. I can never say anything when he's around. I nod and try to look alluring.

Greg punches Andrew on the arm lightly. "Hi, Andrew, old buddy. How ya doing?"

He smiles at me. "Hi, Cassie."

"Look at her red fingers and the pistachio meat in her teeth," Stephie says.

I put my hands behind my back and my tongue over my teeth. I try to imagine what she'd end up looking and smelling like if she fell into a Roto-Rooter.

"OK, kids, enough playing," my mother says as she goes out of the kitchen. "Get all the dishes into the dishwasher so we can leave."

With the coast clear, Greg gives Stephie a kiss. Andrew stands behind them kissing his hand and making faces. It's almost funny, but kind of embarrassing and interesting at the same time.

I clear off the table and pretend not to notice. Terrible headache. It's probably a brain tumor or a fungus that is spreading through my nasal passages.

One of these days, I'm going to get even with Stephie. She thinks she can get away with everything, just 'cause she's so beautiful and successful and a big deal at school and everything. Well, I may not be as beautiful, but I'll show her. She's not the only one who can be somebody. Just wait 'til school starts. I may be somebody too. My friend Vicki's got it all figured out. When she gets back from camp, we're going to put "Operation Overthrow" into action. It's a plan to get the big clique out of power—the kids who always think they've got the *right* to run everything. If it works, things are going to be very different.

My mother rushes in and just misses catching them in a clinch. "OK, everyone, into the car. Stephie, you may drive." Her voice sounds so sweet. That's because of Greg.

The beauty queens get in the front, and I get in the back. Andrew follows. And then Greg gets in. I pretend we're going out for a ride. Greg's the father. I'm his wife and Andrew's the result. Stupid Stephie's the chauffeur. My mother's just along for the ride. We've decided to give her a day away from the old folks' home.

I think about ways to torture people who treat younger sisters like dirt.

We back out of the driveway. I stare straight ahead and try ESP to get Greg to notice my inner beauty.

He says, "Stephie, honey, be sure to start braking for the stop sign."

My mother turns around and smiles. "What a wonderful teacher you are, Greg. I wish I'd had someone like you to teach me how to drive when I was learning."

The car makes a sudden lurch.

It's enough to make me want to throw up. I'm glad when we get to the station. The only thing worse than being with Stephie and my mother at the same time is being with them both with some guy around.

Once we get to the station and on the train, my mother starts reading a fashion magazine.

I stare at a blotch on my hand and decide it's the "heartbreak of psoriasis." I try to imagine what it would be like to be an only child—not the one in the middle, the radish in a bunch of roses.

Chapter
2_____

It's appendicitis or an ulcer. The pains start right in front of Bloomingdale's. I'm never going to look like the mannequins in the windows or the people going in and out of the store.

My mother grabs me by the hand. "Come on, Cassie, let's start by getting some fancy clothes. Now that you're growing up, you'll be going to more parties, out on dates."

Fancy clothes, parties, dates. I'm going to explode, the first teenage bomb in captivity. Dates. The only person who ever asked me out on a real date was Alvin Randall. He asked me to go to the sixth grade spring concert, my first invitation. Alvin carried a walkie-talkie with him all the time. His mother had the other one. She always called him up to remind him to stop at the store, or to get home on time, or just to say hello and tell him how much she missed him.

Vicki says that Alvin is going to end up "neurotic, repressed, and not a very good person to have a relationship with." I just think he's one of the biggest creeps to walk the face of the earth. So I told him that my parents wouldn't let me go out until ninth grade. He told everyone I said that, so no one has ever asked me out again. I doubt if they would have, anyway. Alvin said he'd wait for me. Thank goodness his father got transferred and the whole Randall family and their walkie-talkies moved to Columbia, Maryland. This would have been the year to ask me out again. Yeech.

My mother's pulling me toward the door. "Come on, honey. This is so exciting."

"Mom, I don't need fancy stuff, just regular clothes."

By this time, she's pushed me into the revolving door and is right behind me. I debate letting it go full circle, ending up outside again, but decide against it. Where can I run? She's got the fare home.

I follow her up the stairs and then on the escalator. Looking down, I see all these women descending like locusts on the makeup counters.

I look up at my mother. She really is beautiful —striking, that's the word most people use for her. Red hair, green eyes (but somehow she manages not to look like a leprechaun), fantastic figure— she looks real young. She says I look more like her father's side of the family. Needless to say, none of them are stunning. I sometimes think I wouldn't mind looking the way I do if everyone else in my family didn't look so much like models. I try to imagine her getting sucked inside the escalator when it reaches the top.

She has been talking a mile a minute since we entered the store. ". . . I really wish I were just starting high school . . . I missed so much. . . . What with your grandparents being so sick . . . and then when they died . . . getting married . . . I really do wish I could start over. You're so lucky to have your whole life ahead of you."

I just nod and stare at the blotch on my hand. It's probably a contagious, fatal rash caused by the red dye on pistachios.

"I hope your asthma gets better this year," she continues. "It makes you sound so bad. Don't get me wrong, darling, I don't mind taking care of you when you're sick. It's just that when you're not, I get tired of having to contend with your hypochondria."

Hypochondria. I get so sick of being called a hypochondriac. She gets me so confused. Sometimes I think she likes me better when I'm sick. Sometimes I think she hates me when I'm sick.

As we stand at the clothes rack, she pulls out all these skirts for me to try on. I pull out one from the rack that I really like. It's a patchwork wraparound.

"Cassie, dear. That's not you, not you at all. You need a waist to wear that."

Everyone looks at me—the teen-totem. My stomach feels queasy. It's bubonic plague, legionnaire's disease.

I put it back. "Look, Mom. Let's try this stuff on. Please." I just want to escape.

We each carry clothes into the dressing room. Everyone there looks as if they've just stepped out of *Vogue* or *Cosmopolitan*. I feel as if I've just crawled out of *Mad* magazine.

"Darling, try those on. I'll go into the room next to you and put these on. Just something to keep me busy while we're getting you clothes."

Ten minutes later, I own two new skirts, one beige and one blue print. My mother gets four— navy, striped, glittered, and plaid.

The shirts come next: four for me and five for her.

"Isn't this great fun, Cassie? Don't you just love it?"

"Mom, can I get some blue jeans now?"

We go to the dress department. I get a denim jumper. A compromise. She gets one too. Repulsion.

On the way to the shoe department, she says, "Bet you didn't expect all this for your birthday IOU."

She's right. When I got the IOU certificate on August 18, I didn't expect it. What I was hoping for was a silk screen and other art equipment. But I guess my mother wouldn't have liked that as a present for me. She wouldn't have been able to buy herself four tubes of paint for every two she bought me. The only painting she does is her toes and fingernails. She never puts up any of the paintings I do; she says they're "too modern for her decor." If I ever have kids, I'll put up anything they create and be real proud of it.

She looks at me over the sweater counter. "Don't slouch. Your shoulders'll get rounded. You look as if someone pushed your knees in."

I close my eyes and try to vanish. Maybe I can get some tropical disease that will make me waste away to nothing.

She walks over to me. "Your hair could use a rinse, to give it highlights. I think that will help."

Help. She makes me sound like a lost cause. The brain tumor starts pounding in my left eye. But I don't say anything. She'll only get mad and tell me how ungrateful I am. How lucky I am to come from a nice family, one that cares for me. That she only says what she does because she loves me. And who else, she says, would tell the truth but someone from the family?

By the time we get to the shoe department, I'm wiped out. And worried about what my father's going to say when the bills come in. I hope that my father understands and still loves me.

Last stop, jewelry department. My mother tries on African bead necklaces. I walk over to the other side of the counter and look at earrings.

Some guy walks up and starts to examine the necklaces. He's fantastic looking, like a movie star, has teeth that belong in a television commercial. Maybe he'll notice me.

He turns to my mother. "That looks terrific on you."

She smiles. "Thanks."

I think I'm going to die, right here, right now.

"How about a cup of coffee?" he asks.

She smiles again and then looks over at me. "I'm sorry, but my sister and I already have plans."

I drop an earring on the floor and bend down to look for it.

"How about your phone number for another time?" he says.

Why doesn't he notice her wedding ring? Doesn't that make any difference in New York City? Why was I born?

He shrugs his shoulders. "You don't know what you're missing," he says and walks toward the gourmet food section.

"Cassie," my mother says with a grin, "let's go to lunch."

I nod and say very loudly, "Yes, *Mother*."

Frowning, she walks out the door.

I follow. Again, there's no choice.

Once we sit down and order, she says, "Why are you angry, because someone made a pass at me? That happens, you know. I never get involved. So what's the problem?"

I say nothing.

She says, "That man paid more attention to me than your father has recently. You know, I thought I did the right thing when I married him. My parents were dead, and I felt all alone. Your father loved me and wanted to take care of me. I don't know what happened, why it all changed."

I feel awful. Don't know what to say, so I push the wrapper back on the straw, scrunching it up like an accordion. Then I put the wrapper on the table, fill my straw with coke, and let out a drop on the wrapper. It looks like a snake moving. Maybe it'll bite me and I'll die a terrible, slow death.

My mother continues, "All my life I've had to take care of someone. My parents . . . you kids. I guess I really don't know who I am."

What am I supposed to say? It's not fair to mention us kids. We didn't ask to be born. I didn't ask for the asthma. I certainly didn't ask to have an older sister. Anyway, she's beautiful. If I looked like her, my life would be wonderful.

"Look, Mom, I'm sorry I called you 'Mother' in front of that guy."

She smiled, "Cassie, the whole thing was kind of funny."

"Well, I'm sorry . . . and I'll try not to get sick so you have to take care of me."

Her jaw dropped. "Honey. I didn't mean that. Look, I'm sorry when you get sick . . . for you. But I love to take care of you. It makes me feel needed."

I want to cry. I knew I didn't want to go shopping.

She says, "It's just that I was married at eighteen

. . . had Stephie at nineteen. I'm thirty-six . . . that's half my life."

She's like one of those dolls: you pull the string, and the doll says the same phrases all the time. They should market a doll just like my mother. I'd buy one, cut the string on it, and stick pins in it.

I try to cheer her up. I feel it's my duty. "Mom, for me to say that I've been married for half my life, I would've had to get married at six and a half."

It works. She laughs and changes the subject. Saved.

If I'm not adopted, I wish my parents would put me up for adoption. There's got to be some place that's perfect for me. I'm not sure what it would have, but I'm sure what it wouldn't have—fighting, unhappy parents, Stephie, canopied beds that I didn't pick out, or want, and pistachio nuts that won't open.

Chapter 3

We walked into the house carrying the packages and ran into my father, who was polishing his golf clubs. He took one look at all the stuff we bought. That's all it took. I immediately ran upstairs, dropped the packages on the floor, and threw myself on my bed. That's a tradition—throwing myself on the bed when I'm upset and angry. Now I'm lying here considering suicide. That's a tradition too.

World War III is now taking place downstairs. In history class last year, we talked about conscientious objectors during the different wars. That's what I am in this house—a conscientious objector—I think I'll write to the President to ask him to declare a truce.

Maybe if I kill myself, it'll be best for everyone. Probably nobody'd even notice. Not much would change. Andrew will still be the youngest. He might even miss me. Stephanie will still be the oldest. She'll be very glad. My mother will have to find another excuse to go shopping. She'll probably decide that Groundhog Day is a good substitute.

I should do myself in. Throw myself out of the window. Slit my throat so that the blood drips all over the bedspread that my mother chose for me. I could stick my head in the oven. None of those methods will work. My room is only on the second floor . . . I can't stand the sight of blood . . . and we've got a radar range, guaranteed to broil me in a minute and a half. If only I could stick my entire body in so that the door could close. But I can't, so it won't.

I'll hold my breath. Suffocate. That'll show them. I arrange my wishy-washy hair on the pillow, cross my hands across my almost flat chest, and start to hold my breath.

They'll all be sorry. Stephie will atone for the rest of her life by never going out on another date. And her whole face will break out in a pox and her bust will shrink. My father will visit my grave daily and spend at least half an hour talking to me, as if I could really hear. He'll even give up golf. My mother will realize I wasn't so plain after all and will say things like, "If only she'd lived, she'd have been the most beautiful of all." Greg will simply crumble and realize that he made the wrong choice. He'll leave immediately for a Tibetan mountain top. Vicki, a future psychologist and my oldest and dearest friend, will write "The Case Study of Cassie S., Adolescent Suicide." Andrew will miss me the most, but they'll buy him an orangutan to replace me.

Why can't things be the way they were when I was a kid, when I thought it was all OK. That my parents would always take care of me. Now I'm not so sure they can take care of themselves.

Holding my breath isn't working well enough. There must be a leak somewhere because I still can breathe.

I just know what my funeral will be like. Mother will order lots of flowers, and she'll rush right out to Bloomingdale's to buy me a beautiful long white dress. People will say, "What a shame. She should've worn that at her wedding." Mother will wear a very stylish basic black dress, suitable later for cocktail parties. Stephie will probably come in her cheerleader outfit, if she finds time to show up at all. The principal of my new school will hold a special memorial assembly, and all of the students will feel terrible because they never got a chance to vote me into office.

I'll never see another sunset, know if "Operation Overthrow" would have worked, never know what real love is, and never find out if Harry divorces Marcia and moves in with Jean on my favorite soap opera.

I'm growing so fast. I bet my parents will have to buy an extra-long coffin.

The hiccups start. I can't even kill myself right. Half the time I can't breathe, and now I can't stop breathing.

There's a knock on the door. I lay my head back

on the pillow and try to look tragic. I hiccup. It's very hard to look tragic when you're hiccuping.

"Cassie, can I come in?"

It's Andrew. I hiccup again and stare at the ceiling. He comes running in, takes a flying leap, and lands on my bed. "Hi. Want to walk Snurful with me?"

I try to sigh, and hiccup instead. "Look, Andrew, tell Snurful to go walk himself. Do me a favor—go away. I just want to die."

"If you die," he says, "can I have your stereo and your hair dryer?"

"Why the hair dryer?" I ask.

"To use on Snurful, after I give him baths."

I grab my pillow and whack him over the head. "Come on, Andrew, I'm counting on you to be one of the few people sorry to see me dead."

He jumps up and down on the bed as if it's a trampoline. "Cassie. I'm only kidding."

I grab him by the leg to stop him. "Andrew, cut it out. Act your age."

He looks right at me and grins. "I am. I'm seven."

"Did you have a nice time at John's?" I give up trying to reason with him and decide to hold off on death for a few more minutes.

"No. His mother bought one of those things that sets off an alarm when he starts to wet the bed. John's afraid to go to sleep . . . thinks he's going to be electrocuted. So he stays up all night. He fell asleep on the floor while I was there."

My mother yells up, "Come on, kids. Time for dinner."

I guess World War III's at recess so they can get enough nourishment to keep fighting.

"Andrew, tell her I'm sick, can't make it to the dinner table."

"But Cassie, you always make me do that."

"Come on, Andrew, I'll give you a quarter if you tell her."

"Make it fifty cents."

"Thirty-five. Last offer. Take it or leave it."

"Sold." He shakes my hand and leaves.

What a little crook. He says he's saving it so that if he has a family someday, there won't have to be any fights about money. Either that or he'll buy a Shetland pony. He's not sure which.

My father comes up a few minutes later. I was sure it would be my mother. "Cassie, what's wrong?"

"I think it's pneumonia from the air conditioning at Bloomingdale's." The second I mention the store, I want to bite my tongue. "Daddy, I'll take back the stuff if it'll make you happy."

He shakes his head. "No, honey, you need new clothes. It's all right. Not your fault. Just another thing for your mother and me to fight over . . . It's not your fault. I love you very much. We're just going through a bad time right now."

I want to ask him if he's going to divorce us, but I'm scared of the answer.

He kisses me on the forehead and leaves.

Sometimes I think my parents are wonderful, and sometimes I hate them. I wish I could make up my mind.

My mother brings up a dinner tray. "Cassie, I really wish you'd eat dinner with the family instead of getting sick whenever there's the slightest problem." She sets the tray down in front of me on the bed. A hot dog and bean casserole. Disgusting. It's always her answer to last-minute meals. I personally would prefer a beef potpie, but she's always saying that frozen foods prove that some mothers don't care enough to spend time making food for their families. Vicki says that's one of the most unliberated things she's ever heard. Anyway, it's a lousy casserole. Vicki's mother makes a much better one, with brown sugar and mustard. My mother just throws it all together, and then talks about how it shows this incredible love.

I stare straight ahead and pretend she's already gone. I can hear her voice saying, "You are one of the most unappreciative children I've ever known. See how I fight to get you decent clothes. And this is all the thanks I get."

After she leaves, I wait until the spots before my eyes go away. Then I get out of bed, pick the pistachios out of the dried-flower arrangement, take the carpet lint off them, and try to relax.

I wonder how Lizzie Borden felt when she was growing up, and whether she was guilty of chopping up her parents. Soon I start to daydream about how it's going to be when I escape from this zoo. One of these days, I'm going to move into New York City, go to the Art Students League, really learn how to paint. I'll get an apartment in the Village or Soho and never have to eat my mother's hot dog and bean casseroles.

I'll get memberships to all the museums and spend lots of time in them, learning about art by looking at the masters and listening to all the lectures. I'll become the best artist that I can. All of the New York galleries will fight over the right to show my work.

People will contact my agent from all over the world, trying to purchase my work. Royalty will beg for paintings to hang in their castles. They will invite me to private audiences and parties. I will only go if they clean all the crocodiles out of their moats.

I will become Andrew's guardian, send him to the best schools, buy him his very own zoo and a gold-plated shovel to clean it up.

And I'll open my very own school, one that lets kids feel that they are important, that admits that kids have problems and rights too. I'll pick all of the teachers myself.

When I grow up, I want to be happy. I don't think that's asking too much.

I think I'll buy shares in a pistachio nut farm. That way I'll never have to stay up late at night, worrying about bad crops, rising prices, or hoarders.

Sometimes it's easier for me to live in dreams than in the real world.

Chapter 4

Phones that ring first thing in the morning drive me up a wall, especially on a Sunday morning. I'm too tired to answer it, but I'm afraid it might be important.

It's rung seven times and either stopped or someone has picked up another extension. Maybe it was a radio station calling to ask me what's my favorite station, and if I answer right, I'll win a trip to one of the islands.

There's a pounding on the door.

"Answer the phone, you little creep. It's for you," Stephie yells. "Don't you have any normal friends who call at decent hours?"

I hope she hits a cement wall when she goes for her driving test. As I reach for the phone, I look at the clock—eight forty-five—a little early, but no reason for name calling.

"Hello, Cass. It's Vicki."

"Fantastic! When did you get home from Camp Genius?"

"Camp Palmer. Don't tease me."

Vicki gets embarrassed about her high IQ and how her parents are always sending her places to "keep her mind active."

"When did you get home?"

"Late last night. Cassie, guess what? I met someone at camp. I'm in love."

In love. Vicki always gets everything first—a high IQ, a bust, a boyfriend.

"His name's Kris. He wants to be a political activist, too. And he's the most wonderful person in the world."

"What's he like?" I want all the details.

"Brilliant, socially aware, tall, thin, great smile, wonderful sense of humor. And he's older—fifteen."

"Is he a sex maniac?" When I say that, I want *all* the details.

"Don't be silly," is all she says about that. "We promised to write every day."

"Where does he live?"

"California."

Well, now I don't have to worry about her spending all her time with him. California to New Jersey's a long way.

"Cassie, how've you been feeling? Any more physical manifestations of your psychological problems?"

"What?" Here we go again, my not always understanding her.

She says, "Have you been getting physically sick over things that are bothering you?"

Oh, that.

"Well?" she asks.

"I guess so. I just hate to talk about it." I can feel the asthma acting up a little and hope she won't notice the wheeze if it starts.

"OK, we'll talk about this later. Right now, I'm calling everyone up to meet for 'Operation Overthrow.' "

"Oh, already? Before school starts?"

"Sure," she says. "I figure the sooner we start, the better. If we get everything planned initially, we'll have time for the campaign and to start off our freshperson year well academically. And you know that big group of over-inflated cgos will run for office, as usual, and do nothing for the whole class in terms of politics."

"Well, I just wonder if it's such a good idea."

"If you're finking out on this, Cassie Stephens, let me know now. I've got to be prepared. You know you'll be the best choice. Enough people like you, no real enemies, good enough grades. And you don't threaten people, make them feel uncomfortable, the way I do sometimes. So you're the best choice. But if you don't want to do it, tell me now."

Vicki's got a way of making me feel that I should do something. That it's good for me and I should get over being scared. I'm scared but try to get over it. "No, I want to do it."

"Good. Well, listen, I'm going to call up the rest of the kids and invite them to a combination organization/return-to-school party. Can you help set it up? About three?"

"Great. I'll be there."

Stephie picks up the extension. "Listen, *moron*, I've got to call Greg. Get off!"

I yell, "You get the hell off this phone, turd face! You've got no right to butt in . . ."

"Up your nose with a rubber hose," she screams back and slams down the phone.

"Sometimes I'm glad I'm an only child, although sibling rivalry might be interesting to experience," Vicki says. "That was awfully rude, though."

"And not too original," I say.

Vicki laughs.

"I hate her," I say. "She thinks she's the greatest thing in the world. You don't know how lucky you are to be an only child."

We finish talking, and I get off the phone and lie there having a nervous breakdown. Vicki'd say it's only an anxiety attack, but I know it's more serious—caused by my sister and thoughts of the impending election. I suppose I could've said no, but she's my very best friend, and since she wants to be a psychologist, she's having me be her first patient. I need all the help I can get during these, my formative years.

Finally, it's breakfast time. Sunday is the one morning we all have to eat together. One by one, everyone straggles into the dining room. Nobody looks overjoyed about being there.

It's practically ninety degrees, but Stephie's wearing a turtleneck with her shorts. That's a dead giveaway. She's hiding a mark on her neck, I bet. A "hickey," I once heard her call it. Sometimes I think Greg must turn into Dracula when the moon is full.

Everyone sits down and starts buttering their toasted English muffins. Except Andrew. He spreads mayonnaise on his and then sprinkles cinnamon and sugar on it.

My mother says, "Let's do something as a family today."

Andrew says, "Sure," and puts more catsup on his grape jelly and eggs.

"Damn it, Anne," my father says, "why don't you let me know ahead of time? I already made a golf date with Henry Watersford."

Stephie shakes her head, adjusts her turtleneck, and says, "Greg and I are going over to Cindy's to swim. Why can't we get our own pool? It's the end of the year. They must be having sales now."

"You certainly are your mother's daughter sometimes—sales, swimming pools—do you think I'm made of money?" My father shakes his head.

"I don't think it's fair, bringing me into this," my mother says, raising her voice. "I didn't say anything."

It's time for me to make a fast exit. I can feel an attack coming on. "Look, I don't feel well," I say. "I'm going to go back to bed."

My mother says, "See. All I want is for this family to do something nice together, and look what happens."

My father slams down the pitcher of orange juice. "Don't blame me. You could have given us enough time to plan."

At that point, I rush upstairs. I don't know what to do. I want to run. But where? I want to be on somebody's side, not to feel so alone. But whose? I'm starving, but can't go back down there. It's too early to go to Vicki's. I'm so upset I can't even see straight to read anything.

I've got to calm down, try to stop the asthma attack from happening. The doctor says calming down will help, and the medicine too. I take some.

It takes a while to work, to make me stop feeling that I'm going to drown. I'm always afraid that this time it's not going to work, that I'm going to choke on the gunk in my lungs.

I sit down and try to think calm thoughts. I pretend I'm at a museum in Paris and this guy comes up to me while I'm painting. It's a special exhibit of talented new artists, and I've been chosen to represent the United States. This guy comes up and falls in love with me. At first, I tell him that I must devote my entire life to art, but then I fall for him and elope, planning to spend the rest of my life as a starving, but loved, artist. It turns out that he's a prince, and he takes me to a castle to live happily ever after. I also sell a lot of my paintings and contribute to the upkeep of the castle.

I invite my whole family to come over for a visit, but Stephie's got to sleep in the coal bin.

I'm calmer now. I pick up the phone to call Vicki. Stephie's on, talking to Greggie-Poo, and she yells, "I'm talking, ugly, get off this line."

I'm getting out. That's it. Going to Vicki's early. She won't mind. At least there are some places outside where I'm accepted.

I look at myself in the mirror. There are going to be lots of people at Vicki's later. I should try to look human. Blue jeans, sandals, a striped T-shirt. I almost look human. People may even think I am. I don't feel that way though. Vicki's always saying that I "internalize all the things my family says I am, that I let them define me rather than making up my own definition for who I am." She says that I am prettier and brighter and more talented than they can admit, too. But I think Vicki just says all that so I don't feel so bad. I mean, what are best friends for?

I grab my knapsack and rush out of the house, yelling, "Going to Vicki's house. Won't be back until tonight." I've got to move fast so no one's got a chance to say no.

Rushing down my block, I feel as if I've escaped from the loony bin.

"Hi, Cassie. How've you been?" Stan Harrison stops his bike.

Why do I always have to run into him? He never takes a bath. He asked me to come over to his house last year to see his stamp collection. I told him I'm allergic to the glue they put on the backs of stamps.

"Hi, Stan. I'm fine. What's new?"

"New York . . . New Jersey . . . New Hampshire . . . that's what's new." He pushes his glasses back up on his nose.

Why do I always get the creeps? I almost wish this one had a walkie-talkie with a mother attached to call him home.

"Stan. Gotta go now. See you around. Bye." I rush off.

When I get to Vicki's, her mother lets me in. "Cassandra. Wonderful to see you. Vicki's upstairs . . . on the phone, as usual."

I wave and rush upstairs. Vicki signals that she'll be off the phone in another three minutes. Knowing her, that means another eight.

Sitting down on the floor, I empty out my knapsack.

Might as well straighten it up while waiting— comb, brush, lip gloss, ticket stubs from the last movie I saw, two paperback books, my wallet filled with pictures of everyone from eighth grade graduation, no money, my small sketching pad, a Hershey bar wrapper, several pens, my sunglasses, Kleenex . . .

Vicki hangs up. She looks great. Suntanned, pretty, a T-shirt that says "Uppity Women Unite."

"Hi, Cass. You're real early. What's happening? I'm glad to see you, but I didn't expect to for another couple of hours." She comes over and we hug each other.

She sits down, and I throw everything back in the bag but the Hershey wrapper. "Fighting at home."

"Should have guessed. Why don't you join us for brunch?"

Food at last.

We sit down with her parents. Nobody fights at the Norton house. At least not while I'm there. Vicki says that they do fight sometimes, but that it's psychologically healthy to air feelings honestly. I don't know if my family does it honestly, but if awards were given on the basis of yelling, we'd win the Mental Health Award of the century. I guess we'd probably be disqualified, though, on the basis of lack of sanity.

After brunch, we sit around, and Vicki and I plan out some of the campaign posters. I love doing stuff like that.

The kids start arriving at three. By four, there's a real mob.

I've got to hand it to Vicki. She's got representatives from all the groups at school. Also some of the people who are sort of strays.

Vicki stands on her Ping-Pong table. "Can I have everyone's attention, please," she yells.

People continue to talk.

She cups her hands and screams, "Attention please," and breaks into a tap dance.

Everyone laughs and then quiets down.

"Now that I've got your attention, I'd like to explain our strategy. As we all know, the same group of kids always run the school. They're only nice to all of us at vote time."

"Yeah, the rest of the year they act like snobs," yells Harry Baker.

People are nodding their heads.

"And they don't do anything for all the people," Vicki states. "Just for themselves and their friends."

More nodding.

"So," Vicki continues, "I think we should all unite and pick a common slate of people to run. Kids from different groups, different backgrounds. Then if we all vote as a block, we can get the people we want into office, the people who will do something for the *entire* class."

Still more nodding.

"I think we should write up a list of offices, what the requirements are, and what people should be considered," suggests Bobby Crowell.

Vicki says, "Good idea. How about president first?"

First. Easier said than done.

Everyone has definite ideas about what type of person should be chosen.

If we took all the suggestions made, the president would have to be a conservative, liberal, militant. He or she would have to be an intellectual person, who doesn't act too smart and who is committed to support of the arts, sports, and keeping things the way they are, while making drastic changes.

For a while it doesn't look as if we're going to get anywhere. Finally Vicki says, "Enough is enough. If this plan is going to work, we've all got to make some compromises. We've got to choose someone bright and articulate, interesting but not too far out—a person who gets along well enough with teachers, without getting along *too* well. We also have to make sure the person does well academically and cares enough about all the people."

People are nodding.

"So I think we've got a pretty clear-cut choice," Vicki says. "I nominate Cassie Stephens."

Before I know what's happening, someone seconds it. The vote's taken. I'm chosen.

It's the first time I've been nominated to run for anything since fifth grade. That was for safety-patrol captain. Steve Farber won. He made everyone salute him. Then they were all sorry, but it was too late. I'd already been scarred by the agony of defeat and vowed never to run for anything again. So here I am setting myself up for it again. Running for president. I ought to have my head examined.

The rest of the decisions come easier.

Tony Amato is chosen as the vice-presidential candidate. He's super bright, always has a major part in school plays, and acts friendly to lots of different types of people. He could be in the big clique, but he says that as a group, "they're boring elitists."

For recording secretary, it's Joey Steinberg, and for corresponding secretary, Andrea Smith. That way the slate is equally balanced—one male and one female.

Amanda "Cheapo" Turner is selected to run for treasurer. She was the junior high math whiz and has also saved every allowance she's ever gotten since she was eight. She's a living legend: "Saving it for a rainy day." When that day comes, she'll be able to buy an ark.

Class representatives—Vicki Norton and Jerry Martin. Lots of people wanted Vicki for president, but since she feels that a feminist future-psychologist will be more effective as a representative, that's what she got. Jerry Martin is one of the nicest people in the world. Stephie once said, "He's got a face that only a mother could love." First of all, I don't know how she can say that, given our family. My mother certainly doesn't love Stephie's pretty face. Anyway, Stephie's got a heart that only a witch could adore.

Then Vicki says, "Now that we've got our slate, we need a platform. Since Cassie's going to be our next president, she should lead us."

I'm stunned but stand up. It wouldn't look good for the presidential candidate to pass out in front of her constituency. As Vicki gets off the Ping-Pong table, she flashes me a "You can do it" smile.

I get up on the table, sure that it'll collapse under me, leaving me with a broken, shattered body that can only be replaced by bionics.

The table holds up.

So do I.

The kids start applauding.

I smile nervously and feel like a clod.

"Thanks. I hope we win and show everyone that all people are important and deserve a voice in government." I feel as if my face is frozen into a smile and wonder if this is a medical condition peculiar to all politicians.

There's still applause.

I raise my hands and motion for quiet.

Since I never wanted tap lessons, I took ballet. I go through the basic ballet positions. Everyone takes the hint and quiets down.

I sit cross-legged on the table. Standing up in front of a group is not easy for me. Don't know where to put my hands and arms, how tall to stand—stuff like that.

The suggestions begin. It's not so rough, at least not now. I call on people, listen, make some comments, let majority rule. It's actually kind of fun. Maybe that's because I'm a Leo, and we're supposed to be leaders.

Looking at everyone, I see a new kid. He's definitely cute. Vicki probably imported him from an outlying suburb to act as mediator if candidate negotiations failed.

I try to look nonchalant and absolutely interested in what Douglas Long is saying. "We should have a TPA back-to-school night."

"Explain."

He grins. Sometimes Douglas acts as if he's been smoking oregano leaves. "You know how teachers are always telling our parents about us. Well, we should have the teachers' families come in and tell them things about the teachers. How they're not working up to potential, how they spend all their free time in the faculty room drinking coffee and gossiping with the other teachers instead of learning new stuff. How they can't keep their mouths shut in class, don't return papers on time. We can also tell the good things, if there are any."

More applause. And a lot of yelling. A bunch of rowdies. I love it.

While I'm trying to decide whom to call on next, I see Freddy Patterson standing behind Lois Andrews, trying to sneak a snap at her bra. Freddy's got a minus IQ; he owes a couple of points to whoever passes them out.

I pretend not to see and get more suggestions.

Coffee for all people, not just teachers, is one. "Men" and "Women" signs on the bathrooms, instead of "Boys" and "Girls," is another.

Some of the kids want courses in the following subjects: comic strip heroes and antiheroes; skin care; disco dancing; the care and feeding of problem parents; decaling, tie-dyeing, and batiking T-shirts for fun and profit; the rights of children and young adults; and rock stars of the century.

Somebody suggests that the school rent out a classroom to McDonald's to compete with the cafeteria.

The most reasonable proposal is to allow students to help run the school, to make decisions that affect all of us.

We decide to play up the parts about fair representation for all, about students' rights and responsibilities, and then we decide to call it a day and put on some music.

I get off the table and feel good, as if it was an OK beginning. I still don't know whether I'm "presidential timber." I feel more like presidential balsa, or maybe plywood.

Someone has put on records.

I notice that even though Vicki has left her heart with Kris, the California genius, she doesn't mind dancing with Harvey Kaplowitz. Sometimes I think I'm a monster, jealous of my own best friend. Everything comes easy for her—nice parents, good dancer, nice body, smarts, gets along better with people. She's my best friend—how can I be so envious?

"Hi, Cassie." The new guy comes up to me. "My name's Bernie Howard. I'm Vicki's new neighbor."

Wow. He's not a mediator. He's here to stay. I hope I can talk to him without wheezing.

"Hi. What grade?"

"Ninth. A new vote for you."

The election. I forgot. I look at him. He's a

little taller than I am—hazel eyes, beautiful eye-lashes, sandy brown hair—really cute. I'm not too crazy about the braces, but other than that, I think he looks wonderful. On a scale of one to ten, I give him an eight—to be changed to nine and three quarters when the hardware comes off. It's not that braces are so terrible, it's just the way they sometimes gets gobs of food caught in them. His are clean, though.

"Would you like to dance?" he asks.

"Sure."

We start to dance, and I guess I'm doing all right because he doesn't step on my feet or collapse from laughing.

After the song ends, I smile and say, "Thank you, sir," with a curtsy. I saw that once in an old movie.

We laugh at the same time.

"Bernie, how long have you lived here?" I ask. "What do you like to do? How does Vicki know you?" I also want to ask if he's a boy scout doing his daily good deed by talking to me, but I don't.

"We moved here two weeks ago from Michigan. I like to do lots of stuff . . . want to be a veterinarian someday. Vicki called this morning when her parents told her I existed as a next-door neighbor. So here I am. I'm glad she called. Do you know how boring this town is, not knowing anyone?"

"I can imagine. I know how boring it can be, knowing everyone."

He grins.

"Why'd you move?" I ask.

"My father got a teaching job at Rutgers. So we moved here. What about you?"

"I've lived here forever. And I'm an artist. If you want to be a veterinarian someday, I have a house full of animals you can practice on—a garter snake, a sheepdog, two flying squirrels, and Stephie."

"What's Stephie? A cat?"

"Sort of. She's my older sister, a senior."

He laughs. "I have one like that myself. She's a senior too. Maybe that was a bad year for the birth of sisters."

All of a sudden, I realize I've got to go to the bathroom. I always have to go to the bathroom when I get nervous. It's really gross. Everyone used to call me TB when I was younger—Tiny Bladder.

"Cassie, I'll be waiting here."

Waiting here. I feel like the frog that was kissed by a princess and turns into a prince. Except that's a biological impossibility.

I feel silly. Maybe this is love at first sight. I can't get too excited. He's new here, and as soon as everyone at school sees him, he's going to be very popular. He's probably talking to me because he's so lonely. He's even cuter than Greg.

There's a line at the bathroom. It figures. There's always a line when I really have to go. I try to cross my legs, stand there and look natural.

Ginny Rogers comes over to me. "Hi, Cassie."

"Hi, Ginny." We've never been that close. In fact, when we were in kindergarten, she cut off one of my braids. I've never forgotten that. When we took Home Ec sewing last year, I made sure we worked at different tables. No more pigtails, but I don't like to take chances.

"I see you and the new guy are getting friendly." I smile.

"Running for class president, the new guy, your looks . . . bet you think you've got everything." She turns and walks away.

Sara Baskin's on the line behind me. "She's just jealous," she says. "Don't worry about her."

Jealous. That's a shock. Jealous of what? All my life, my mother and sister have told me how ugly I am, how worthless. How can anyone be jealous of that?

When I get into the bathroom, I stare at the mirror. It doesn't say, "Cassie, you are the fairest of them all," but it doesn't break either. Maybe I'm not so bad after all. I always thought Ginny was cute. Now Sara says she's jealous of me. Amazing. Bernie's still waiting for me when I get downstairs. I'm still waiting to turn into a frog.

Chapter 5

The alarm goes off. This is it. School starts today.

I shower and put on one of my new outfits . . . and then take that off and try on another, and another, and another. I finally decide on the denim jumper with the patchwork design blouse. I hope it's OK.

I put on my elephant hair bracelet, the one I always wear on special occasions, when I need luck. I don't wear it too often. I try not to abuse it—first days of school, when report cards come out, when art awards are being announced. So far it's been pretty good. Some nights I lie awake and worry about it being stolen by a burglar.

When I get downstairs, my mother and Stephie are already at the table.

Stephie's blowing her nail polish dry. "Cassie," she says, staring right through me, "I don't want anyone at the high school to know you're my sister. The humiliation would be too great. Don't even act like you know me."

"Don't worry," I yell. "I can't stand you either. I'd rather have King Kong as a sister."

Andrew walks in and sits down. "King Kong can't be a sister. He's a boy."

I eat my breakfast without saying a word.

When I get up to leave, I say, "Andrew, have a great first day of school. Mom, I hope you have a lovely day. Stephie, I hope you get what you deserve."

I leave before she has a chance to say anything nasty, checking to make sure that my bracelet's latched on tightly.

By the time I get to Vicki's house, she's already sitting on the porch steps.

I don't see Bernie. Since he lives next door to Vicki, I thought I might get lucky.

"Hi, Cass," she says. "Great outfit. New?"

I nod. "Part of the Bloomingdale's binge. I love your outfit too."

She's got on a pair of basic blue jeans, tennis sneakers and a T-shirt that says "Ms."

"We better rush, gotta catch the bus," she says.

Rush. I don't even want to go. I hope the school nurse is nice.

We make it to the bus stop just in time to get on the bus. I check to see if Bernie's there. He's not. Everybody's waving to each other and screaming, "Welcome back."

I smile at everyone and make sure that I haven't lost my bracelet yet. I'm going to need all the help I can get. First day of high school, waiting to see if

Bernie's going to continue to pay attention to me. He's not on the bus. Bernie and his family probably decided to move back to Michigan. My one chance for the romance of the century. And now he's vanished.

Vicki and I take a seat toward the back, making sure it's not over the wheel.

Vicki says, "My aunt gave me a new book on family relationships. I've got your problem all figured out."

I whisper, "Tell me . . . quietly."

She whispers back, "What's happening is a classic case of psychological child abuse, a condition prevalent in many middle-class homes. No one ever physically touches you, but you get caught in the middle, feel ambivalence, experience sibling rivalry. You'll probably bear psychological wounds for the rest of your life. Your ego and id are not strong."

Neither is my stomach. I feel ill.

The bus pulls up to the school.

"I think I'd better go home . . . don't feel well," I say as we get off. "It's probably botulism."

Vicki pushes me inside. "Cassie, you *are* going to class," she says. "Come on, remember, you've got to be healthy for the election."

Before I know it, I'm standing in front of my homeroom door and Vicki's on the way to hers. I look around trying to figure out how to escape. I'm sure Stephie's right—that I'm this big drip. Not even my father says anything very positive, so it must be true. There's only Andrew—he thinks I'm beautiful. He also thinks Mutant is beautiful.

A teacher comes out and takes the schedule out of my hand. "Stop loitering. You're going to be late. Do you belong here?" He looks at the schedule. "You do. Well, come in. Do you need a special invitation?" He shoves the schedule back in my hand.

I follow him in. No escape.

He stands there while I take a seat. Then he walks out again.

I look around to see if I know anyone in the room. I do. I wave and act as if I belong. They wave back.

The teacher comes back in. On the board he writes MR. STODDARD. Then he turns and says, "Class, that's my name. Mr. Stoddard. *Mister*. Make sure you get the pronunciation right. It is now eight thirty-two. You will be seated by this time each day or be marked late and sent to the office for a late pass. Perhaps word has already spread about me. But for those who haven't heard, I won't tolerate any nonsense. If we are going to get along this year, you must follow *my* rules or you will be very sorry. *Very sorry*. At eight thirty-two, in your seats. At roll call, say 'present' or get marked absent. Nothing else will do, not 'here' or anything else. You've just gotten to school, so no bathroom passes. I want total silence when I take attendance, when we say the Pledge of Allegiance, and when we listen to the loudspeaker for announcements. Anyone speaking at these times will be given detention. At eight forty-seven, you file out of here by row, silently, making sure the desks are left in a straight line. I run a tight ship. Get used to it."

Someone raises her hand. "Can I sharpen my pencil?"

"You probably *can*, but you *may* not. You should have done that before the bell rang. And get rid of the gum."

Then he passes out an insurance form and tells us to sit quietly until the bell rings. I sit there and read the pamphlet. There's certainly nothing better to do. The form's incredible. If I lose both hands and both feet, I get $7,500; the entire sight of one eye—$1,000; one hand and one foot— $7,500; one hand *or* one foot—$2,500; my life— $2,000. You have to be careful. It can't add up to more than $7,500. Also, they won't pay if it happens during brawling or war (declared or undeclared) or as the result of ptomaine poisoning. They also won't pay up if it's a suicide.

The bell rings. We all jump up. Mr. Stoddard makes us sit down again until he excuses us. Then he makes sure that all the desks are lined up evenly; that no one's taken the flag or the pencil sharpener; that there's no gum under the desks; and that there are no scraps of paper lying around.

As he lets us file out, one by one, he says, "I'll have all of you trained by the end of the year."

I'm definitely sick by this time.

Then Bernie walks in and says, "Sorry I'm late. Here's my pass."

"When you speak to me, young man, refer to me as 'sir.' "

I stand outside the door, making sure that Bernie comes out of this alive. He's nodding.

"I said call me 'sir.' "

Bernie nods, "Yes, sir."

"Well get out, now. My class is arriving. I don't need any stragglers from homeroom."

As Bernie walks out, with his back to Stoddard and facing me, he crosses his eyes and sticks his tongue out. I'm careful not to laugh until we get far enough away from the room.

"Hi, Bernie. Welcome. What happened to you this morning?"

"Overslept. The whole family overslept. What a way to start the first day."

"I was afraid that you might have been taken as a hostage on a flying saucer."

"I was. My return and the safe return of my family was dependent on my agreeing to be in that creep's homeroom. What's his story anyway?"

I shrug. "His name is Stoddard. That's about all I know. Except that I think he would be a perfect match for my sister."

"What a lousy beginning." He frowns. "But you're in there, so that makes it better."

The toad turns princess again.

We look at each other's schedules and see that

our only classes in common are art and English. We've got to rush off in our separate ways.

I've got Mr. Meyerson next. Algebra. He hands out books. Mine looks as if it's been through three wars. He tells us there's not going to be any bathroom passes since we all had time to go during homeroom. Wonderful. Just what my tiny bladder and I need to hear.

He begins teaching.

I personally think all math teachers buy their clothes with the chalk dust already on them. Either that or they buy them clean and immediately step up against a blackboard, like the way lots of kids step all over brand-new sneakers to get them to look old. I also personally think that math stinks. I can't do it. Artists shouldn't have to take it if they don't want to. Meyerson the Messy is too fast. If I ever need to know anything about the dumb subject, I can use a calculator or hire someone.

In history class, we have to write about "The American Who Means the Most to Me Historically." Definitely one of the dippiest assignments I've ever gotten. I write about Lizzie Borden.

Gym class next. Finally a class with Vicki. We compare notes. None of her teachers are very exciting either. Not yet. We're told to have our names sewn on the pockets and backs of our gym suits, name tags in our socks, our names magic-marked on sneakers. I'm surprised we don't have to have our names tattooed across our foreheads.

When the roll is called, the teacher says, "Cassie Stephens, any relation to Stephie?"

What now? I hate to lie, but Stephie said not to tell anyone that we're sisters. "We are very distant," I say. That's true enough.

"Are you planning on trying out for cheerleading?"

I can feel myself blush. "No." Stephie'd never allow it. Anyway, I could just see me start a yell and end up being carried off the field with an asthma attack. My special cheer could be "Let's have a wheeze."

Vicki and I walk out when the bell rings and head to lunch. No wonder the insurance policies don't cover ptomaine poisoning. Someone must have tasted the food in our cafeteria. I'm going to have to get used to it. It's dumb, but nobody I know "brown bags" it anymore.

During lunch, Vicki and I plan strategies for trying to reach all the kids in the freshperson class. We decide to have each of the officers-to-be approach and talk to a section of the class—everyone, including the kids in the "in group," unless we're running against them. Not an easy assignment, but if we say we're going to reach everyone, it's the only way to do it.

Lunch period's the shortest of the day. It figures. Vicki and I have to leave quickly to make it to our next classes.

Sara Baskin's in the class. "Hi, how's it going?" she asks warmly.

"OK, but I've got a homeroom teacher that's a cross between an orangutan and a dictator."

"Stoddard?"

"How'd you guess?"

"He's a living legend around this place. My brother, Tommy, had him. He's never been the 'best,' but a couple of years ago his wife and kid were killed in a car accident. He's been a beast ever since."

Bernie joins us at the table. He's frowning. In fact, he looks absolutely furious. "Just got detention for running in the hall. Definitely not my day. I'm beginning to really miss the old school."

"I'm sorry," I say.

"Not as sorry as I am. It's Stoddard who got me. I've got to stay after school, looking at his rotten face for a half an hour."

"It could be worse," I offer. "It could be an hour."

"True." He grins. "And he could be twins. You're right. I'm definitely in luck."

We laugh.

The teacher walks in, writes "Ms. Larson" on the board, and explains what the mini-course is: "This class is a study of the history and trends of art in this country. I hope that you all enjoy it."

It sounds great. She seems just the way I'd want an older sister to be. She smiles a lot and listens to us when we say something.

Then she says, "I want to get to know each of you quickly. So I want to try something. Each of you say your name and the names of the people before you. Please, begin." She points to Jackie Davids.

"My name's Jackie Davids."

"Next," Ms. Larson says.

I don't know the next person.

She smiles shyly. "I'm Pam Markowitz."

"Hi, Pam. You should also give the name of the person before you."

So that's how it's going to be. Wish I were first.

Sara's next. "I'm Sara Baskin. This is Pam Markowitz and Jackie Davids."

I'm tenth. "My name is Cassie Stephens." I point to each person before me. "Bernie Howard . . . Sandra Portee . . . um . . ." I have to think a minute. "Lisa Greer . . . Fay Hunter . . . Carl McElroy . . . Patty Smithson . . . Sara Baskin . . . Pam Markowitz . . . Jackie Davids." I made it without an asthma attack.

Ms. Larson's last. "I'm Ms. Donna Larson. This is Lenny Silverman . . ." She works her way back to Jackie, missing about seven names. She remembers mine though. What a relief.

By the end of the period, we're all laughing and it's like we've all known each other forever. When the bell rings I'm disappointed. I could spend the rest of my academic life in this room, learning from Ms. Larson.

English class next.

Bernie's in that class too. We walk there together. I feel as if everyone's watching. I daydream about how we'll be elected class couple by our senior year.

We pass Stephie and Greg in the hall. Even though we pretend not to see each other, I can tell that Stephie's surprised to see me with Bernie. Maybe I should have bought some turtleneck sweaters during the Bloomingdale's binge.

As soon as we sit down in English class, Mr. Martin, the teacher, calls the roll. When he gets to my name, he says, "Cassandra Stephens."

"Present."

"Do you know the legend of Cassandra?"

Oh, no, not again. And this time in front of Bernie. Why me? Will it never end?

Once he shows off his outstanding knowledge of Greek mythology, Mr. Martin calls the rest of the roll and then writes on the board: "Humor is emotional chaos, remembered in tranquility. James Thurber."

He says, "I want a writing sample from each one of you. Explain the quotation and give an example from your own life." Then he sits down as if he's real proud of the assignment.

I stare at the paper. Something terrible at the time, but funny later—the time in fifth grade when the elastic on my underpants broke and they fell down while I was at the blackboard doing a math problem. Too embarrassing. I thought I was going to die at the time. I don't want anyone to remember it and start teasing me again. Everyone called me "D.D." for months—Dropped Drawers. I cer-

tainly don't want to remind everyone of that again.
And this guy looks like the kind who reads papers
out loud to the whole class.

Instead, I write about the time I baked my first
cake. Put all the ingredients into the bowl, turned
on the electric beaters, lowered them into the bowl.
It took forever to get the mess off the ceiling.

Bernie walks me to my last class and then leaves
for his. I'm sure that the second he leaves me, he's
going to run into someone whom he's immediately
going to fall in love with and forget that I even
exist.

Last period. Study hall. Vicki's in there, too.

It's in the auditorium. Seems like a million
people are in there, including Mr. Stoddard. Just
when things were getting good. He makes it very
clear that if we so much as open our mouths, he'll
ram his fist down them.

One of the kids asks someone to lend him a pen.
Mr. Stoddard starts yelling and gives him an assignment to write. "The only proper way to talk in
class is first to raise your hand and seek permission
from the instructor in charge. Then, and only
then, speak your piece to the fullest. All other
methods eventually lead to chaos."

"Chaos" again. It figures.

Stoddard says, "Write it twenty-five times. Open
your mouth again, ever, and I'll double it and keep
doubling it until you learn to keep your mouth
shut."

For the rest of the period, no one says a word.

I think about how Stoddard's got his own problems, which I should try to understand. But it's hard.

When the bell rings, Mr. Stoddard has everyone file out.

By the time Vicki and I get out, we've really got to rush to make the bus.

We just make it. I sink into the seat, look for Bernie, and then remember his detention.

Vicki plops down. "Only one hundred and seventy-nine to go," she says, pretending to faint.

Chapter 6_____

Getting home, I expect to have my mother at the front waiting to find out about my day.

What I find is a note saying that she's out shopping. Drat.

All the way home, I thought about stuff to tell her: how some kids had mugged the principal in the hall and gotten ten books of late passes; how the janitor ran off with the school crossing guard; and how the entire student body nominated me for Prom Princess.

I go upstairs, change, take off my jewelry, and stare in the mirror. Why can't I look better? How can I keep Bernie interested? How can I win an election? Maybe when my grandmother asks me what I want for Christmas, I'll tell her plastic surgery. That would really be good. A smaller nose, less freckles, tinier ear lobes.

I continue to stare at the mirror. My grandmother is always saying how wonderful I look. She'll never agree to the surgery.

How depressing—Stoddard; a sister who pretends I'm not alive; a mother who only deals with me when we're shopping or when I'm sick; a father who never has time for me; a face that looks so ordinary. I can't stand it.

Even my eyebrows are weird—bushy, sticking out, and no space between them. How could I have gone thirteen whole years and never noticed? Nobody told me.

I go into my parents' bathroom and take the tweezers out of the medicine chest. I've seen my mother do this for years. It'll be a breeze.

Attack a clump of hair in the middle. The eyes water. Forgot the cream . . . get that and start again . . . start on the right . . . go to the left . . . back to the right eyebrow . . . it doesn't look real even. Go back to the left. Stephie and my mother never end up looking like this. I hardly have any eyebrows left, just red marks that look as if they're going to scab. It looks terrible. Maybe excess plucking can be hazardous to the health. It's time to stop now.

I look at the mirror. It's awful. But I can't stop now. I better shave my armpits and legs to practice for when they get hairy.

Armpits are easy. The left leg's not going so well. I think I've taken off the top layer of skin. It's pretty bloody. Maybe this will be the end. It's not deep, but it's awfully messy. I wonder whether the insurance policy will count this as suicide.

A car door slams and the front door opens. With

any luck, it'll be my mother or father, not Stephie. She and Greg are probably off making out somewhere anyway.

"Mother?"

"Yes, Cassie?"

"Come here quick!"

I hear her running up the stairs. "Where are you?"

"In your bathroom."

She rushes in, takes one look at my leg and kneels down. "What happened?"

"Shaving." I cry.

"You're going to be all right." She puts a towel on the leg.

"Am I going to be scarred for life?"

She shakes her head.

"Do you think I'm going to need a blood transfusion?"

"Cassie, calm down. You're all right." She goes to the medicine chest and takes out a white stick that looks like chalk. Wetting it, she rolls it over my leg. Torture. I'm burning up. Then she sprays some first aid stuff on.

She hugs me. "Cassie, you're all right now. I think everyone goes through something like this. Don't worry, honey." She goes to kiss me on the forehead. "Oh, no!"

"Does it show that much?"

She nods and shakes her head. "Honey, you could have asked me. I would have been glad to help you out."

I start to cry. "I'm not going outside till it all grows back."

"Cassie, that's going to take a while."

"I don't care. They can get me home tutoring. They gave it to Jennifer West."

"Jennifer got home tutoring because she was in a body cast, not because she tweezed her eyebrows off."

I continue to cry. "They can put me in a body cast, just so no one ever sees me like this." I think of Bernie. How's he ever going to fall in love with a girl with a bald face?

"Cassie, now stop that crying. I know you're upset, but it's not the end of the world."

All this wouldn't have happened if I hadn't taken off my lucky bracelet.

And to top it off, I can't eat pistachios in front of her.

"Come on, honey. I'll try to fix it." She works on them for a few minutes. I can tell by the way she's shaking her head that it's no use.

She gives me another kiss. "Don't worry. It'll grow out." She smiles.

"Don't laugh at me. It's not funny."

"I'm not laughing at you. Look, someday this will seem funny to you. It's not a tragedy."

I think of the composition that I had to write in English about humor being emotional chaos remembered in tranquility. I'm never going to be calm enough to think this is funny.

"I've got to go downstairs to get dinner going," my mother says. "I'll send Andrew up to keep you company."

She leaves and a minute later Andrew and Snurful come in. He looks at my face and falls down on the floor, laughing hysterically. Just what I need. My foot in his stomach is what he needs.

"What's so funny, *you little creep*?"

He keeps laughing and pointing.

"Tell me or get out!"

He tries to stop laughing. "Remember the time we went to the butcher shop?"

"Yeah?"

"And I saw the chicken without its feathers."

I remember. He had asked, "Why is that chicken naked?"

"Well that's what you look like—a plucked chicken." He starts to giggle and roll around on the floor again. Snurful thinks it's playtime and starts barking.

"Andrew, stop that or I'll cut you into little pieces and flush you down the toilet."

He clucks.

"I'm not kidding. I'm going to step on your face if you don't shut up. You too, Snurful."

I look in the mirror. I personally don't see anything funny about it. I look like I've got leprosy. I probably do have leprosy or face rot. Maybe my face will start to fall off, and they'll see it was better to have a plain face than no face at all.

My mother walks back in. "Here, Cassie, these

are for you." She hands me her pair of sunglasses that I've always loved. She's never even lent them to Stephie.

I put them on and look in the mirror. They cover my eyebrows and half my face.

Andrew clucks again. I ignore him.

Andrew says, "Mommy, doesn't Cassie look like a plucked chicken?"

She starts to laugh. I start to cry again.

"Cassie, now calm down. There's no need for all this. You are one of the most melodramatic children I've ever seen."

Andrew clucks for a third time. He's really asking for it.

She puts her arm around me and says, "Let's go downstairs. You can help with the dinner."

I go downstairs. Still no chance for even one pistachio.

Andrew follows, still making chicken noises.

I turn and say, "Chickens *destroy* gerbils. If you do that anymore, you know what's going to happen to Mutant."

He pretends to cry.

When we all get to the bottom of the stairs, my mother says, "Listen, children. Enough is enough. Let's cut out this squabbling."

"Mom, Andrew . . . promise not to tell Stephie when she comes in from cheerleading practice."

"For a dollar." Andrew makes a quick recovery from his tears.

"Andrew, you are *not* blackmailing your sister."

She's really coming through for me today.

She nods. "I wish you and Stephie could get along. But since you don't, I guess it's not wise to give her anything to use against you."

I can't believe it. Maybe the way to get her to be really nice is to keep myself messed up.

Andrew and I set the table and then since we've got extra time, he invites me out to his tree house. That's a big deal, since it's his own private place. He and Daddy made it this year. My mother hates it, says it's dangerous. Personally, I think she hates the fact that Andrew can escape.

We climb up the ladder and sit down.

"Want M&Ms?" Andrew asks, pulling out a bag from an old cigar box.

I think of how much my mother would yell about it spoiling our dinner and nod yes.

"Andrew, how do you feel about our family?" I ask.

He shrugs and rubs his nose. "I wish we all liked each other. There's too much fighting. On all the TV shows, everyone makes up at the end. We don't."

"Does it make you unhappy?"

He tosses an M&M into the air and catches it in his mouth. "No more talking about it or I'll make chicken noises. Want to play Monopoly?"

I nod. "Why not?"

He gets the game out, sets it up, and says, "You be the banker."

By the time we get called to dinner, he owns Boardwalk and Park Place (with hotels on both of them), all the railroads, the utilities, and almost everything else. I'm wiped out. I *never* should've taken off my lucky bracelet.

At dinner, Stephie says, "How come Cassie gets to wear those glasses and you won't let me?"

"They're your mother's," my father says. "She's got a right to do what she wants with them."

"How come she's wearing them to the table?" Stephie's acting nicer now because she doesn't want to get him angry at her.

Ignoring her, I say to Andrew, "Please pass the butter."

Giving up easily is something that Stephie doesn't do. "Is this the ailment of the week for our resident sickie?"

Let her make fun of me. See if I care. I hope she gets rabies from Greg.

"Drop it, Stephie," my father says.

"As if I don't know," she smirks. "You should've tweezed out your midget mind as well."

"Who told you?" I yell.

"You just did, nitwit. Lucky guess." She giggles.

"Enough," my father says. "And you better not tell anyone else if you ever expect to use the car when you get your license."

She shuts up.

I hope she flunks when she goes for her license, runs over curbs, and hits the markers.

I keep thinking that if Stephie's guessed, so will the rest of the world.

After dinner, I go upstairs and check in the mirror. The eyebrows still haven't grown back.

Every time I look in the mirror, I want to puke.

Chapter 7

In the morning, I check on my eyebrows again. No change. A little more scabby maybe, but not better looking. The leg still looks as if a lawnmower went over it, but I can cover that up with pants. And my armpit looks as if it's got creeping crud rash and it burns when material touches it. But I can hide that too. However, the eyebrows are awful. TERRIBLE.

I put the sunglasses on.

After I get dressed, I go downstairs.

Queen Jr. has already left—she's got an early student government meeting. I've got to pick up a petition so that I can show her she's not the only one who can win elections. I hope.

Andrew clucks hello.

I want to push his face in the plate.

"Mom, this time I think I've really got to stay home. I think I'm coming down with athlete's foot of the face."

"Cassie, you're going to school. Got that? To school, Cassandra Stephens."

"But Mom."

"Don't 'but Mom' me. You're going to school. And that's final."

There's no getting out of it. I say good-bye and head over to Vicki's. Maybe she won't notice.

The first words out of her mouth are: "Hi, why the sunglasses? It's going to rain today."

"Promise not to laugh?"

She nods.

I take off my sunglasses.

She laughs.

The sunglasses go back on.

"Cassie, that's what you get. You're a victim of the mass media's attempt to make all women conform to the same image."

"And you're going to be the victim of a sharp right hook if you don't shut up."

She smiles.

"Oh, Vicki, what am I going to do?"

"Maybe you can get eyebrow wigs at Bloomingdale's. I'm sure your mother will be glad to take you."

I ignore that. "Think I can put eyebrow pencil on it?"

"If you want infected scabs."

Just what I want, an oozing face.

We rush to the bus stop. I stare straight ahead and act as if it's perfectly normal to be wearing large sunglasses on a very cloudy day.

Bernie is waiting at the bus stop. I can see him from a distance.

So does Vicki. "Look, Cassie, if you want to sit with Bernie, I'll understand. If Kris were here, I'd be sitting with him some of the time. It's natural to form relationships. And I think Bernie's nice."

I answer, "I'm glad you feel that way, but not today. Once my eyebrows grow back in, maybe I can sit with him. Until then, I'd rather keep a distance."

"You definitely are an interesting case. Your avoidance tendencies are incredible."

"So are my eyebrows," I whisper.

Bernie's talking to Mark Becker. He looks up, waves, but doesn't come over. They look as if they're into a big discussion. What a relief! Maybe by the time they're done talking, the hair will have grown back.

Once we get inside the bus and sit down, I whisper to Vicki, "Do you think everyone can tell?"

She shakes her head. I remain quiet for the rest of the ride, trying to will my eyebrows to grow back immediately.

When we pull up at the school, I say, "Vicki, I better get to the school nurse. I think I've got polio."

She shakes her head.

"I better go to the school nurse. I'm serious this time."

She shakes her head again. "It's not going to work."

"But I've got it. I can hardly move my legs."

"No. You know it's nerves. They'll just call your mother and she'll tell them what happened."

Vicki's right. No escape. What I've got to do is get through today. That's going to be the worst.

I stop in the girls' room, or as Vicki says, the women's room, and go into one of the stalls. Taking the compact out of my purse, I check them out. Still not grown in.

I've got to rush so I'm not late for Stoddard. On the way, I look for Bernie. I'm not sure whether or not I want to see him up close. At least, not in this condition.

I slide into my chair and pretend to be engrossed in my algebra book.

There's a tap on my shoulder.

"Young lady, I suggest you take off those glasses. You're not in the sun." Stoddard is standing right there.

"I can't."

"What's your name?"

Staring straight ahead, I say, "Cassandra Stephens, sir." Maybe saying "sir" will help.

No luck.

"Well, Miss Stephens, I said take off those sunglasses."

Very softly, I say, "No," and shake my head.

Someone giggles.

"In this room I happen to be boss."

I stare straight ahead.

"If you don't take them off, you'll have to see the principal."

My eyes start to tear.

"I'm waiting."

Everyone's staring.

I pick up my books and walk out.

Bernie's just walking in as I walk out.

I could die.

Mr. Stoddard comes to the door and yells, "If you take off those ridiculous glasses, you may return to the classroom."

Looking around, I see a lot of people. Bernie is looking confused. If I take off the sunglasses, everyone's going to see what I've done to my face. If I don't, it's the principal's office.

The principal's office. I head downstairs. The first floor, that's usually where they keep principals. I've got to ask directions from some teacher who's standing out in the hall looking official.

When I get to the office, I walk up to the secretary and whisper, "Can I please see the principal?"

"What? You've got to speak up," she yells. "I can't hear you."

I feel as if everyone is looking at me again. I just hope the sunglasses are hiding my eyebrows.

I raise my voice a little. "May I please speak to the principal?"

"Why?" she asks.

"Mr. Stoddard says I have to." I want to die, to vanish from the face of the earth.

"I'll tell Mr. Zimmerman you're here. Your name, please."

"Cassandra Stephens." I feel the need for pistachios.

She picks up the intercom: "Mr. Zimmerman, Mr. Stoddard's sent another student to see you." She puts the phone down.

A man comes out of the office. He's smiling.

The secretary says, "Mr. Zimmerman, Cassandra Stephens."

He shakes my hand. "Come into my office."

I should have a heart attack. That would save me.

I follow him into his office.

"Now, what seems to be the problem?" he asks.

I start to cry. "Mr. Stoddard says I've got to take my sunglasses off . . . and I can't. But he wouldn't let me stay with them on . . . said I had to see you . . . so here I am." I keep crying.

Mr. Zimmerman says, "Cassandra, calm down. It's going to be all right." He looks like my grandfather, kind of chubby and bald, with a real nice smile. "Now, were you rude to Mr. Stoddard?"

I shake my head no.

"Is there any medical reason why you're wearing them?"

Maybe I should tell him I have this strange allergy to the light bulbs in the classroom and my eyes turn yellow. But then I'd be stuck wearing the glasses for all four years of high school. And anyway, he might not believe me. So I decide to level with him.

"Promise you won't laugh?"

He nods.

I take off the sunglasses.

Of everyone, Mr. Zimmerman's the best. No laugh. Just this really strange cough. But no laugh.

He looks at me and smiles. "I remember the first time my oldest daughter did that. Only she also gashed her leg."

"Me, too."

He laughs.

I begin to feel a little better. Maybe I should ask him if he's got any pistachio nuts.

"Cassandra, I'll tell Mr. Stoddard I've given you permission to wear sunglasses, and I'll write a note to any other teachers who ask you to remove them, although I doubt any others will do so."

"You won't tell them why, will you?"

He shakes his head.

"Mr. Zimmerman, can you put me in another homeroom? Please."

"No, I'm afraid not."

I put my sunglasses back on. "But he hates me now."

"What if everyone wanted to leave?"

"Maybe then he'd be a little nicer."

Mr. Zimmerman shakes his head again and gets up from the chair. A signal to leave.

I get up. "Well, thanks for not yelling at me."

"Cassandra, it's nice meeting you. I hope there'll be no problems. Let me know if there are."

I walk to the door.

He walks out with me and helps me get a late pass for algebra.

When I get there, everyone stares.

I sit down and someone whispers, "What happened?"

Before I have a chance to say anything, Mr. Meyerson, the math whiz, turns around. "Whoever's talking, get up here and do number three on the board, and get it right or you've got detention."

The kid who was talking to me gets up and puts the problem on the board.

For the rest of the period, we learn more about algebra than I'll ever want to know. I'll never understand why colleges require junk like that.

When the bell rings, a whole bunch of kids crowd around me and ask what happened.

"Mr. Zimmerman says I can wear them."

Everyone applauds.

For the rest of the day, a lot of people come up to me, even Stephie.

"Cassie, what's happening?" she smiles.

"Who are you?" I smile back.

There are a whole bunch of people standing around me.

She pulls me over to the side. "OK, Miss Smart Aleck, what's this all about? How dare you do that in front of other people?"

"You told me never to acknowledge you at school. Right?"

She punches me on the arm. "Cassie, you know I was just joking around. Listen, a lot of kids at this school hate Stoddard. You've won out against him and everyone's noticing you, and people are coming up to me to find out what's the story. Come on," she whispers in my ear, "I'm not going to tell anyone the real reason you're wearing those things. So you better be nice to me." She smiles and puts her arm around my shoulder. It must look good to everyone else. What I feel is my arm getting all black-and-blue from the pressure.

"Stephie, just leave me alone," I whisper. "You never act nice to me. Go away now."

She smiles at me and says very very quietly, "You better reconsider your attitude . . . or else I may rat on you."

I whisper back, "And lose your driving privilege? Ha!"

"I'll talk to you later," she says.

I decide that I'd better be nice to her. If she ever decides to tell on me, I'm a goner.

"Bye, Stephie. See you later."

She grins and waves good-bye.

So that's it. *Everyone* hates Stoddard, and now plain nobody Cassie Stephens has beaten him. Not bad. But what am I going to do next?

By lunch time, I've started calming down, but everyone else is still making a big deal out of it. I'm actually a celebrity. That's what happens when you go to a small school in a small town. Word gets around fast.

Rochelle Wagner comes up to me while I'm standing at the counter putting catsup on my hamburger. "Rumor has it that you're going to run for class president."

I nod.

"So am I."

I nod again, careful that my sunglasses stay close to my face.

She says, "Really, Cassie, I hate to see you build your hopes up. No one's ever beaten our group. We do such a good job. We never forget the little people who elect us." She tosses her long brown hair.

I wonder how to spill catsup on her and make it look like an accident.

She continues, "I'm sure you'll see it our way."

I can't believe it.

"Cassie, why don't you come to a party at my house this weekend. We'd love to have you become part of our group. We were going to ask you earlier." She looks so sure of herself.

"No thanks, Rochelle. My election committee is meeting that night. Thanks for the invitation though. And Rochelle . . ."

"Yes?" She looks floored that anyone wouldn't accept her invitation.

"When my slate gets elected, we'll consult your group, too, to see what it wants. We are the party of *all* the people, you know." I feel powerful and scared at the same time.

She leaves.

I go back to the table and tell Vicki what happened.

"Amazing," she laughs. "The nerve of those creeps. Come on. Let's go get our petitions. Eat fast."

After lunch we go to the student council office.

"Oh, you're Cassie Stephens," says the guy in charge. "I'm Gene O'Connor, student council president. I heard what you did, standing up to Stoddard. Every kid who's ever had him thinks it's great. He's a terror. Guess you won't be afraid to stand up to the administration if you're elected. Good luck now." He smiles.

As we leave with the petitions, Vicki says, "That clinches it. You're a winner."

"How do you know?"

"When the student council president knows a lowly freshperson, that's a good omen."

"It's kind of silly."

"It's very silly," she says, "but I bet it'll get people's attention. Once we have that, we can dazzle them with our platform."

Absolute strangers say hello to me in the halls.

The sunglasses are the clue, I guess. I do notice that there are a few other people who've put on their sunglasses. Just a few, though.

Art class. Bernie's standing outside the door.

"Hi, Bernie." I feel a little uncomfortable. How am I going to explain it all to him?

He walks up to me and says, "Will the mystery guest please sign in?"

He's holding an eraser, but he's pretending it's a microphone.

I speak into the eraser, "I just want to thank all my fans for showing up at my movie premiere."

"Ms. Stephens, would you like to tell those self-same fans why you are wearing those huge sunglasses?"

I have to think fast. "Because the bakery was out of cheesecake."

Got him. He starts to laugh.

Ms. Larson comes out. "How do you expect me to teach without an eraser for the blackboard? Is this the day to 'get the teachers'?" She's smiling, so I don't think she's serious.

Bernie hands the eraser to her. "Ms. Larson, a little elf was walking out of the classroom, trying to abscond with your eraser. After a bitter battle, I managed to retrieve this very necessary teaching tool. I somehow knew it was your favorite eraser."

Ms. Larson asks, "And what happened to the elf, Bernard?"

"I decided to show my humanity and decency and give him another chance. After all, he was very short, but had a wife and eleven children to support. I thought you would understand."

"Yes, I understand perfectly. The next time you want to borrow my eraser, just feel free to ask." She heads back inside.

Bernie whispers, "I was sure she'd fall for that story."

"I'm beginning to think that you're not quite stable psychologically." I grin. "Perhaps you ought to become Vicki's second patient."

"Who's her first?"

"You're looking at her."

He laughs. "Are you a walking advertisement?"

"Yes. Do you think I should sue for malpractice? Don't you think I'm the picture of mental health?"

"It's the sunglasses that prove it."

"I thought they gave me just the right touch."

"Are you going to tell me now why you're wearing them?"

"Sure, a little elf told me to."

Ms. Larson sticks her head out the door. "I hate to break up your rendezvous, kids, but I've got a class to teach. And I'm sure you don't want to miss my pearls of wisdom."

We walk in. Everyone's staring at me, at us.

We listen as Ms. Larson shows us some examples of early American folk art.

When the bell rings, Bernie and I get up. He puts his arm around me and says, "Well, would you allow me to escort you to English class?"

"I'd rather go to Paris, but I suppose English class will have to do, as long as you give me a guided tour."

He does give me a guided tour. "And this, Cassie, is a teacher on hall duty. To your right is a locker. To your left, a water fountain. Under your feet, the floor." He continues like this all the way to English class. I pretend to be a very impressed tourist.

I'm in luck in English class. The teacher is showing a great film, *Why Man Creates*. Not only is it wonderful, but the room is kept dark. People can't try to sneak looks behind my sunglasses.

At the end of class, Bernie whispers, "Cassie, want to go to a movie Friday night?"

I nod. Can hardly believe it. Maybe I should ask him to write it down so that when I get home, I'll have proof that he really asked me out. That it's not all a figment of my imagination.

Study hall. Scary. Stoddard again. He's going to kill me. Everyone thinks I'm this great heroine, but I'm just this scared little kid with a bald face.

Vicki meets me in the hall.

"I can't go in, Vicki. I'm going to go to the nurse's office and tell her I have cramps."

She whispers, "Cassie, you can't do that. If you use that excuse until your eyebrows grow back in, they're going to think you're some kind of medical oddball or something. Anyway, it's not a feminist response. Come on, you've already won."

At this point, who cares? I just know he's going to embarrass me to death somehow. . . .

Vicki smiles. "Come on, Cass, I'll protect you."

"I can't do it."

"You've got to—the bell's going to ring." She grabs my arm and drags me inside.

We sit down just as the bell rings.

Everyone's looking from Stoddard to me. It's the first time I've seen him since I got thrown out of homeroom.

He stands there and glares at me without saying one single word.

The room is silent. No one says a word.

He takes out his roll book and starts taking attendance.

Vicki sneaks me a note. I open my notebook and put it in there, as if I'm studying.

It says, "Looks like you're going to survive. I think he's going to leave you alone. Congratulations."

I smile. Hooray for the good guys, or good persons, as Vicki says.

When the bell rings, I walk out quietly. There's no reason to take chances.

On the bus, we grab our favorite seats. Two days and we've already staked out favorite seats.

We look at each other.

"Only one hundred and seventy-eight days left," Vicki says.

I smile. Maybe the next one hundred and seventy-eight won't be as terrible as I thought they were going to be.

Chapter 8_____

      Practically every student in the entire school wore sunglasses for a couple of days after my run-in with Stoddard. I was sure Mr. Zimmerman would blame and punish me, but he said he's used to fads. One year the students pasted little metallic stars all over their faces. Another time just about everyone wore two different shoes to school. Mr. Zimmerman said there are more important things for a principal to be concerned about.

      Everyone was talking about me, about how brave I was and why I was really wearing the sunglasses. Then Sean Barker shaved his head and pierced one of his ears with two holes. Everyone's paying more attention to him now. He should have pierced his brain.

      We've followed our initial campaign plan. Everyone who's running on our slate had to talk to a specific number of freshpersons. At first, I was really nervous, but most of the time it turned out well. I got to know some people much better.

It's hard being out there, though; "vulnerable" is the word Vicki uses. Running for office means that more people get to know you. It's great when they like you but very difficult when they don't. It's like working hard on a painting and then showing it to people. Criticism's not always easy to take. Sometimes I feel as if I'm walking a tight-rope without a net. It seems as if there is a bunch of crocodiles down below just waiting to get me.

One of the good things about the election is that Bernie and I are working on the campaign posters together. It's been lots of fun, although it's impossible to get him to color inside the lines. The posters look great—colorful, funny. We even did some in day-glow paint, but the janitor wouldn't install black light in the halls.

Things aren't going too badly in some ways.

But at home, whenever no one else is around, Stephie refers to me as "Tweezer Twerp." At least she doesn't say anything about it at school.

Stephie and my mother keep teasing me about "my sudden popularity," how "cute" it is. They tease me about the election and Bernie. I hope the crocodiles eat them.

The movie that Bernie took me to last night was dumb, but we had a great time. Aside from the dumb games I used to play, like post office, he gave me my first kiss—my first real kiss—and my second and my third.

With the election coming up tomorrow, my nerves are shot. I wish it was two days from now. I can't take the suspense. My nails are chewed all the way down. Rochelle's nails are beautiful. She'll win for sure if people look at our hands. She's also started a vicious smear campaign: says I'm absolutely radical, antischool, and plan to bomb the building if elected. It's all lies. Vicki says not to worry, that people know it's not true, but it might actually get us a few extra votes from the maniac fringe.

Speaking of bombing, World War III's still going on at my house, worse than ever. When Bernie picked me up for the movies, they were yelling at each other. They stopped long enough to meet him, but it was obviously a bad scene. I could have perished from the embarrassment. It's awful. I try not to have friends at the house when I know both my parents will be around. Andrew even asked if he could move into his tree house. It's gotten that bad.

My asthma's not getting any better, worse in fact. I'm using my medicine almost all of the time. I hate to put all those chemicals and stuff into my body, but I've got to. It's a matter of survival.

Now I'm sitting here waiting for Bernie to come over again. So far all is quiet downstairs, but I never know how long that's going to last.

We're going over to Vicki's to practice campaign speeches. Bernie is going to be part of the audience. I said we could meet at Vicki's, but then he said he'd rather spend some time alone with me.

Being with Bernie makes me feel less ugly. Vicki says I always was pretty and just didn't know it, that most people feel insecure about their looks. But I know she's just saying that because she's my friend.

The doorbell rings. I rush to answer it. So far so good. No one is yelling.

He's wearing a pair of roller skates and carrying a skateboard. "Hi, Cassie. Couldn't get the car tonight so these'll have to do."

I act surprised and ask, "What happened to the chauffeur?"

"Gave him the night off and the car. He wanted to take his eighty-three-year-old mother to bingo and then bowling." When Bernie smiles, I think he looks wonderful. I even think his braces look wonderful now.

"Didn't he do that last week?" I ask.

Bernie shakes his head. "Last week he took her on a guided tour of massage parlors."

Snurful comes over and almost knocks Bernie over. He's not really the King of the Roller Derby.

Then I hear my mother yell, "Well, if you don't like it, leave!"

My father screams back, "One of these days, you're going to be sorry you keep saying that."

I talk louder to try to drown out the noise. "Bernie, why don't we go for a walk before Vicki's?"

He hands me the skateboard. "Want to race around the block?"

It sounds as if someone's throwing plates.

I'm mortified. Why couldn't they have waited

just a few more minutes. I'm beginning to wheeze.

Bernie says, "Let's go."

I feel frozen, but concentrate on putting one foot in front of the other.

Once we get out to the sidewalk, I get on the skateboard.

Bernie yells, "On your mark, get set, go!"

We race to the end of the block. I win.

"Bernie, I'm sorry my parents are always fighting when you come over." I stare down at the cracks in the sidewalk.

"It's OK. Look, my parents hardly talk to each other. At least yours do exchange words." He shrugs and takes off the skates.

We walk through the park and sit on the swings.

"I'm glad I know Vicki's parents," I say. "They get along. They're normal."

"Who knows what's normal? I always thought parents should take a test before they're allowed to have kids."

"I'd never have been born then," I say. "Look, I don't want to talk about them."

"OK, then will you finally admit why you're still wearing those sunglasses? I know anyway, but I'd like to hear it from you."

"How do you know?" I ask.

"Saw it when I took them off to kiss you last night."

He must eat carrots to see so well at night. Anyway, I thought you were supposed to kiss with your eyes closed.

I blush. How unsophisticated.

He says, "I guess my braces aren't so wonderful, either."

I'm getting embarrassed talking like this. Three kisses and he decides I'm an expert. What does he think—that they give out kissing merit badges in Girl Scouts?

"Cassie, I'll tell you something if you tell me the truth."

"OK, you win. But you go first. And it better be good, Bernard, or I'll put peanut butter in the wheels of your roller skates."

"Promise you'll never tell anybody, first."

I nod.

"Last year, tie-dyeing a T-shirt, I ended up with bright magenta hands. It took a week and a half for it to wear off totally. I wore gloves to hide it, but people thought it was strange since it was July. So I had to live with everyone calling me Puce Paws. It was dumb."

I laugh and say, "OK, I'll admit what you already know. I've tweezed off my eyebrows."

He grins. "That's what most people are guessing anyway."

"What are the other guesses?"

"That Stephie gave you a black eye. I think she started that one."

"The creep!" I yell. "I'm going to poison her dental floss."

He continues, "Another rumor is that you're possessed, and you've got to hide the fact that your eyes are fluorescent and that your parents are saving up to buy you an exorcist for Christmas."

"Where did you hear that one? It sounds like something Andrew would make up."

"He did. Before I rang the bell last night, I ran into him and he showed me all his pets. I bribed him. That's the explanation he gave."

I don't know whether to laugh or to be mad at both of them.

"How much did it cost you?"

"He asked for two bucks. I got him down to ninety-nine cents."

"A real bargain."

"I may lie awake at night and wonder what the two-dollar excuse would've been."

I smile and then remember that Andrew is back home, having to cope with the whole family.

"He also asked me to marry you and adopt him."

"Oh, no. What did you say?" I can feel myself blush. I should have been born pink. It would have saved me the trouble of blushing.

Bernie is grinning. "I told him that where I come from in Michigan, there's got to be a dowry —gifts from the bride's family to the groom."

"What did he say?"

"He said to wait a minute while he thought about it. Then he offered me seven dollars and fifty-six cents, Adam, Eve, Snurful, Fido, Mutant, his yellow yo-yo, two jumping beans, and his electric corn popper—as long as we take him as part of the deal."

"Well?" I ask.

"Well, what?"

"What happened next?"

"I told him we're too young, to keep adding to the dowry and maybe in a couple of years . . ."

"Sexist pig!" I scream. "You should be ashamed."

"Not really. You can ask my family for a dowry. My sister might even contribute to get rid of me."

Andrew and Snurful arrive. Both have lots of hair over their eyes.

It's a public park, but somehow I figure I've got a right to privacy. When you're growing up, there's no place to really get away to.

Andrew says, "Hi, Cassie. Hey, listen, Bernie, I'll throw in my Chinese checkers game."

"All the marbles are missing," I say. "You lost them to John, didn't you?"

He nods. "But the board's still good."

He looks so sad; I decide not to make him feel worse. "Bernie and I have to get to Vicki's, but next weekend I'll do something with you."

"Promise?" he asks.

I nod.

"OK if I join you? We can go to a movie," Bernie says.

Andrew grins. "Sure. Can I go to Vicki's too?"

I shake my head no. "Election stuff."

"I guess I'll go see John," he says.

"Good idea," I say, thinking how bad it must be at home for him.

Bernie and I get up to leave.

"Andrew, want to use the skateboard today?"
Bernie offers it to him.

Andrew nods, grins, takes the board, and scoots
off.

Snurful follows.

I say, "The chauffeur got the car, Andrew the
skateboard."

Bernie hands me a skate. "Put that on. I'll put
on the other one."

We make it to Vicki's. I'm not sure my insurance
plan covers death by roller skate.

Vicki is standing by the mailbox. "Got another
letter," she says.

Vicki's romance is supporting the post office.

"I can't wait for camp," she continues.

Summer seems a million years away.

"Look, he sent another picture."

Vicki's romance is also supporting the photog-
raphy business. This time he's sent a picture of
himself playing tennis.

"He looks wonderful, Vicki."

She gets all dreamy-looking.

"That's a great tennis racket, the best," is Bernie's comment.

Vicki smiles and says, "We'd better go inside.
The speeches need some work."

Speeches in front of the whole freshperson class.
I just know something awful's going to happen;
like the elastic on my underwear going again and
my pants falling down in front of everybody; or
I'll develop postnasal drip and it'll keep running;

I'll have an asthma attack; or my sunglasses will fall off and my nude face will be shown to the world; I'll probably forget how to talk; or I'll goof up my speech. It may be an absolute disaster.

A lot of the kids are already in the recreation room. Kevin Roberts comes over. "Bernie, you going to try out for the football team?"

Bernie smiles and shakes his head. "I don't know who'd kill me faster if I did, the other team or my orthodontist."

Kevin says, "But it'll be fun."

Bernie shakes his head. "If I try out for anything, it'll be for the school play."

Kevin says, "Well, if you're afraid . . ." and walks away.

Bernie looks strange, kind of angry and upset.

I take his hand. "You OK?"

"Yeah."

"Are you sure?"

"Yes."

"Are you really sure?"

He nods.

"Truly sure?"

He speaks real low, "Look, I said I was OK. Now leave me alone. Just drop it."

I drop his hand. I want to cry. Now Bernie hates me. I was just trying to be helpful. Before anyone can see the tears start, I turn and go into the bathroom. At least there no one can bother me.

It's all over. I've gone and messed everything up. Now it's finished. I knew it was too good to last, that I'd do something to screw up. Bernie's going to hate me forever. It's always going to be this way. I'm basically a loser. I don't know why I even bother to try.

I sit on the edge of the bathtub and cry. There's a knock on the door. I ignore it and sit there sniffling.

"Cass, are you OK? It's me, Vicki."

"Yeah. I'm fine."

"Do you want to talk?"

I open the door a little and shake my head yes. She comes in. I sit back down on the tub and whimper. She sits on the hamper.

"Bernie said to tell you to come out, that he wants to talk to you."

"He hates me now. I just know it." More tears. "Why?"

" 'Cause I kept bugging him about how he feels. And he told me to leave him alone." I start really crying.

"But Cassie, it doesn't seem like he hates you, not when he asks me to check on you. He didn't say leave him alone forever."

"But he got mad at me."

She shrugs. "I get mad at you sometimes. You get mad at me sometimes. That doesn't mean we aren't friends."

"But . . ."

Vicki gets her psychiatrist look. "It's just that you don't have proper role models at home. Your parents don't work things out effectively, and they don't encourage their kids to do it either. Somehow they've convinced you that no one's going to care about you but them. It's a very interesting case."

"But my parents love me." I feel guilty if I don't defend them.

She nods. "Never said they didn't, but they haven't given you a whole lot of survival skills."

She may be right. Sometimes I get scared that I'm going to be destroyed. The crocodiles again. I sniffle and start to calm down.

"Do you feel better?" she asks.

I nod. "Yeah, I guess so."

She gets up and looks in the mirror. "How awful. A cold sore's starting. Does it look awful?"

I go over and look. "Vicki, nobody can see it, unless you point it out."

Somebody starts pounding on the door. "Come on, give me a break. I've got to get in there." It sounds like Gary Evans. "My kidneys are gonna burst."

We laugh and open the door. It is Gary.

"Girls. Girls always use bathrooms to talk. I think when you got toilet trained, your mothers spent most of their time talking privately to you while you were on the seat. You see tile and think it's true-confession time."

Vicki turns to me. "Should we leave and let him in after that macho comment or should we teach him the errors of his ways?"

Personally, I think we should let him wet his pants, but I want to talk to Bernie, so I say, "Let's let him in. At least our mothers toilet trained *us*."

We walk out slowly. He rushes in.

Vicki says, "I'm going to check on the food. See you soon."

I go back downstairs. Bernie's waiting by the steps.

He takes me by the arm. We go back upstairs and outside.

"Back in a minute," he yells out to Vicki.

Once we get outside, he says, "Look, Cassie, I'm sorry I told you to cut it out, but I said I was OK three times. You were beginning to sound like my mother."

"I'm sorry too. I didn't mean to bug you."

"It was Kevin, not you. He's always trying to get at me because I'm not great at sports and he is. Guys are supposed to be great at sports and I'm not. I like some sports, but I'm not really good at any of them."

"But you're real good at lots of things."

"But not sports . . . and I don't even like football. That's practically un-American. At least, my father seems to think so."

"Don't worry. I won't turn you in to the FBI." I reach out for his hand.

"Good. Look, we better go back in. You've got to practice your speech. Listen, when you get elected, are you still going to remember the people who knew you when?"

"Like you?"

"Like me."

I nod. "Absolutely. Anyway, I'm probably going to lose."

He leans over and gives me a kiss. Number Four.

"Bernie, know what?"

"What?"

"I'm beginning to like the feeling of steel and wire."

We go back inside.

He laughs.

I practice the speech. It's all about taking stands, allowing for individual differences, and representation of all the people in the ninth grade.

Then I listen to the suggestions and make some changes. Everyone on the election slate does that. Then we put on records and dance.

I keep thinking about how everything's changing, how nothing seems certain. Some things get better. Some things get worse. But they sure don't stay the same.

Chapter 9

Election day and I can't even have pistachio nuts. It wouldn't look right for a candidate to give her speech, smile, and have pistachio meat stuck between her teeth.

I keep changing outfits. My room looks as if a cyclone hit it. Clothes thrown all over the place.

Brown slacks, a camel pullover, brown suede boots, small hoop earrings, a patterned neck scarf. My lucky bracelet. That's it. Just the right outfit for an election. It makes me look kind of competent, and yet not too dressed up in case I lose.

I walk into the hall. Stephie's also out there. "Cassie?"

"Yes." I stare straight ahead, trying to feel strong inside so when she's nasty, it won't hurt so much.

"I . . . um." She stops.

"Yes."

"I just want to wish you good luck today. I know how scared I get when I'm running for something." She looks a little uncomfortable.

I'm in shock. Speechless.

"Well, anyway, good luck. I hope you win." She turns to go down the steps.

"Stephie," I call after her.

She turns. "Yeah?"

"Thanks. And listen . . . I'm sorry about the time I told Burt you stuffed your bra with Kleenex."

She laughs. "Oh, that . . . yeah . . . I could've killed you. But he would've found out anyway. Well, again, good luck."

After she leaves, I just stand there for a minute. Maybe it's an omen, Stephie treating me like a human being.

By the time I get downstairs, she and Andrew are fighting over who gets the last of the milk. I guess people don't change overnight.

I take out a bowl, put cornflakes in it, slice a banana, pour orange juice over it all, and try to ignore the shouting.

My mother's just sitting there, looking exhausted.

"Mom, are you feeling all right?" I ask.

She shrugs and then nods.

"Today's the election," I say.

"I know. I only hope that your health is good enough for you to do well in your school work, be president, and deal with your active social life." She frowns.

"Give her a break, Mother. Just because you're

not happy with your social life, let us have our own. And you should be happy. Cassie's getting healthier."

"Don't you start, Stephie. You and your father think you can treat me any way you want," she yells. "Well, I won't stand for it. Do you hear me?"

"How can I not hear you when you're shouting?"

They keep screaming at each other.

Why can't they stop? Why does the day have to start this way? I feel as if I have to choose sides as usual, to make everything nice.

Andrew is sitting between them, looking back and forth as if he's watching a Ping-Pong game. He picks up the catsup bottle, splatters some over his heart, puts the bottle down, and screams, "They got me!" Then he falls to the ground, with his tongue hanging out of the side of his mouth.

Stephie and my mother stop yelling and look at him.

I start laughing and can't stop. The tears are streaming down my face.

Andrew is moaning and saying, "My last wish is for a truce."

Stephie starts to laugh. So does my mother.

Andrew sits up. "Is everything OK now?"

There's catsup all over his shirt.

My mother says, "I don't know whether to spank you or hug you. Come here."

There's a pause while we wait for the verdict. She reaches out for him and holds him tightly.

When she stops the hugging, there's catsup on both of them.

"I hate it when we all fight," she says. "Look, I want everyone to be here for dinner and afterward."

"What's up?" Stephie asks.

"We want to be with Cassie on election day to celebrate or to make her feel better."

I finish my cereal and say, "Gotta go now," and feel pretty good about the plans. I wish she'd been more sure of my winning though.

As I leave, my mother is saying, "Andrew, go change. I can just see the note I'm going to have to write. 'Andrew is late on account of condiment contamination.'"

Vicki's waiting. "You're running late. What happened? I was afraid you were chickening out, or sick."

"You wouldn't believe it, if I told you."

"Try me."

I try to explain the Catsup Kid and the continuing Stephens family saga.

Vicki gets hysterical when I get to the part where Andrew requests the truce.

"I love that kid. Wish he were my brother," she laughs.

At the bus stop, Gina Crane comes up to us. "You've got my vote. That other group's always been so stuck up. I think you'll represent us all much better."

Janie Eden says, "Me too. Best of luck."

Once we sit down on the bus, I say to Vicki, "That's good, two votes for us."

"Don't be so sure. They're probably telling the other side how much they like them."

"You're such a cynic," I say. "I'd never have thought about that."

"Not cynical. Realistic . . . maybe a little defensive."

"Vicki, I think I'm going to have a nervous breakdown. I should pull out of the race. My mother thinks I'm too sickly to be president."

Vicki sighs, "Cassandra Stephens, your mother's always going to think you're too sickly to do anything. Don't give in to that."

"Vicki, I really don't think I can go through with this. Artists don't become politicians."

"OK, that's it. Now get it all out of your system. Let's just calm down. Write down all your excuses now. Then we'll be done with it."

She hands me her notebook. I scribble for a few minutes. It's hard to write on a moving bus. Plus it makes me carsick.

I hand her the piece of paper with all the reasons listed on it.

WHY I CAN'T RUN
By Cassandra Stephens

I must spend all my time doing the following:
1. my algebra
2. becoming a better artist
3. checking for tooth decay

4. fighting nail biting
5. comparison shopping for pistachio nuts
6. learning how to whistle with two fingers
7. enrolling in a night course in the care and maintenance of eyebrows
8. teaching Andrew how to win back the marbles from his Chinese checkers set
9. organizing my notebook
10. pulling the weeds from around the Venus's-flytrap in my room.

Vicki is laughing. "All out of your system?"

I'm laughing, too.

"Well?"

I nod.

"OK, that's it then. No more talk about not running on the day of the election."

"OK."

The bus pulls up to school.

I've got to go to homeroom, tell Stoddard I'm not absent, and then go to the auditorium. Homeroom is being extended so that freshpersons can listen to the speeches and then vote.

I've managed to keep pretty clear of Stoddard, not say a word to him. I hate to have to tell him anything, to give him the chance to play big deal just because he's the teacher and I'm a kid.

Walking through the halls is a real trip. Lots of kids coming up to wish me good luck. I look at all the campaign posters Bernie and I made, and I feel proud of us.

Martha Gottlieb comes up. She used to baby-sit for Andrew, Stephie, and me when we were younger. Now she's in college, but she's come back to observe the school because she wants to be a teacher. "Cassie," she says, "good luck. I hope you win."

"Thanks."

"I can't believe how you've grown up," she continues. "Last year you looked like a little girl; now, look at you. What a change over the summer. You look lovely—makes me feel absolutely ancient."

"Well, Marth, thanks a lot. I've got to get to homeroom." All this talk about me growing up is making me nervous.

I rush off, going over in my mind what to say to Stoddard.

He's at the door.

I take a deep breath and walk up to him. "Mr. Stoddard, sir, I've got to go to the auditorium right now to get ready for the election speeches. I was told to tell you I'm present and then to go there."

He looks down at me. "Address me first. Then wait till I acknowledge you. Start over."

Start over. I want to kill him, to cry, but instead I stare straight ahead and say, "Mr. Stoddard, sir." I feel as if I'm playing "Mother, may I?"

"Yes, Cassandra. You may speak."

I feel like a dog. Maybe I should roll over and play dead—or beg. But I continue; I've got to get there. "I request permission to go to the auditorium because I'm running for office."

He says, "I certainly hope the best person wins. Rochelle's in one of my classes. She's a good citizen and will do a fine job. Cassandra, you're dismissed."

I leave, thinking about what a rotten jerk he is. How can he always be so mean? Wasn't he ever a kid? I'm sorry that bad things happened to him, but he's always making bad things happen to others.

Everyone else is in the auditorium. I'm trying to think of ways to get rid of Stoddard without getting caught.

Mr. Zimmerman says, "Cassie, we were just getting ready to send out a search party."

"It took a while to get permission to come," I say, hoping to get Stoddard in trouble without mentioning any names.

"Well, you're here now, so let's go over the procedures."

He explains the order, the reps, the secretaries, the treasurers, the vice-presidents, the presidents, alphabetically in each classification.

It's going to take forever to get to me.

After the explanation, I go over to Vicki.

"I'm going to the school nurse," I whisper.

"Oh, no you don't! What is it this time?" She's holding on to my arm.

Brainstorm. "It's toxophilus, I'm sure." I figure I've got her this time.

"*Toxophilus* was a book on archery, written by Roger Ascham in the fifteen hundreds. I read the same encyclopedia when we did the reports on toxins last year. So there."

Drat. Foiled again.

We're seated on the stage. Folding chairs. All of the freshperson homerooms shuffle in and are seated.

I'm glad I wore slacks. Or I'd have spent the whole time worrying about whether the audience could see up my dress.

I sit there, trying to listen to everyone else's speech. I want to win. I'll be a good president. I just don't want to be a wipeout, a failure. How do politicians survive? They must have nerves of steel. I have nerves of Silly Putty.

My turn. I make it to the podium without dying, make my speech.

As soon as I finish, I start to worry. Did I remember everything—the part about how the officers should act as student advocates with the administration and faculty, the need for class unity, at the same time allowing for individual differences? Did I look competent enough? Humble enough?

I ask Vicki as we're leaving the stage.

She says, "You did fine. How'd I do?"

"Fine, but you know you always do."

"Cassie Stephens, one of these days you're going to learn that everyone has hang-ups and insecurities." She shakes her head and smiles.

Back to homeroom.

Time to vote.

I vote for our slate.

People tell me I did well.

Bell rings.

On to class.

Results not in till the end of the day.

I go through the motions.

Classes.

Talk to people.

Kid around.

Everyone keeps saying how calm I am, how good I sounded. If they only knew how I feel.

Vicki and I stand in line for lunch. "Cass," she says, "guess what I brought us?"

"One-way tickets to join the French Foreign Legion?"

"No, better. Look." She pulls two small bags out of her pocket book.

Jelly beans in one bag. Pistachios in the other.

Saved.

Chapter 10_____

The suspense is killing me.

It's so quiet in study hall that I can hear the click of the intercom as it comes on. The announcements begin:

The PTA meeting.

The student council car wash.

A singing ad for the school newspaper.

I look toward Vicki. Her eyes are closed. I know her. She's got all her fingers crossed and her thumbs twined together.

More announcements:

Yearbook pictures.

Reminder—no smoking of any kind on school property. It's grounds for suspension.

Whoever stole all the erasers from room 114 will be punished unless the erasers are returned.

Tryouts for the school play, *Cheaper by the Dozen.*

Personally, I think that any school that does a play about twelve kids in one family likes to use everyone who tries out.

Finally, Mr. Zimmerman's voice comes over the loudspeaker. "Before announcing the results of the election, I wish to commend all the participants. It was a close race. Everyone should be congratulated for their desire to serve the freshman class."

Freshperson, I think.

He continues, "It's now my pleasure to announce the new officers.

"Class representatives: Vicki Norton, Jerry Martin.

"Recording secretary: Joey Steinberg.

"Corresponding secretary: Andrea Smith.

"Treasurer: Amanda Turner."

"Vice-president: Louise Kiernan."

Tony didn't win. The whole slate's not winning. I knew it. Rochelle's going to win. At least Louise is nice.

Mr. Zimmerman continues, "President: Cassandra Stephens."

I won. We both won. I won.

I can't believe it.

Wait till my parents find out. Class president.

Vicki and I take one look at each other and start yelling.

Mr. Stoddard also starts yelling: "Detention. Monday. The two of you."

Everyone gets real quiet. The bell rings and we march out silently. But once we get outside, it's celebration time. Vicki and I are jumping up and down. People come over and jump up and down with us. It's really exciting.

Finally, Vicki says, "Ms. Stephens, we've got to hurry. The presidential bus, Pistachio One, is ready to leave."

While rushing to my locker, I look around for Bernie. No sign of him.

I remember, his appointment with the orthodontist. He doesn't even know that I've won.

The bus is pulling out as we arrive. We flag it down.

The only two seats together are right at the front. We collapse into them.

"I can't believe that fink gave us detention," Vicki says, sticking a piece of gum in her mouth. "Do you think he's human?"

"Doubt it. He's probably a science-lab experiment gone wrong. They didn't want to waste taxpayers' money, so they recycled him for use as a teacher."

She laughs and offers me some gum. I take it out of the wrapper and pop it into my mouth.

I've won. It finally sinks in. Class president. Me. Cassandra Stephens. A winner. Mr. Zimmerman said the race was close. Maybe the sunglasses helped me. Maybe everyone got tired of the big clique. Maybe some people really like me and think I can do a good job. I'm freshperson class president. What an up. I only hope I can do a good job. I hope Rochelle doesn't hate me now. I hate to be hated. Anyway, she's still got longer nails than I do.

I try to pull the silver paper off the white part of the gum wrapper without tearing it, and I think of how proud my parents are going to be.

As she gets off the bus, Vicki says, "Party tomorrow night. My parents won't mind."

They never mind parties. Their only rule is that they chaperon.

"OK," I yell. "See you tomorrow."

Andrew and Snurful are on the porch.

"Did you win?"

I nod.

Andrew keeps screaming, "Yippie!" and jumps up and down. Snurful starts chasing his tail around and barking. I sit down on the porch steps. Andrew keeps jumping.

"Silly, it's not that important," I say.

He sits down next to me. "To me it is. Can I be your press secretary and go on television?"

"They don't do that for what I won."

"Well, can I be your press secretary just in case?"

I nod and reach over to push the hair out of his eyes. He grins. There's a new gap between his teeth.

"What happened to the tooth?"

"It was loose, so Sherry Finklestein and I played dentist."

"Did it hurt?"

He shakes his head. "No . . . she's real good . . . and after it was over, she gave me a toy with the bill."

"How much does she charge?"

"A quarter. We went to the store with it and bought candy to share. The tooth fairy leaves fifty cents, so I make a quarter and had half the candy."

Playing dentist—I remember doing stuff like that when I was a kid. But now I'm freshperson class president. I hope that doesn't mean I always have to act grown up. I hope class presidents are allowed to get sick.

"Let's go in," I say. "Is Mommy home?"

He nods. "Having coffee."

She's at the kitchen table, drinking the coffee and smoking a cigarette.

"Mom, you quit," I sigh. "Put that out. It's not healthy."

"I'll do what I want. Don't bother me. I'm your mother. You're not mine."

I can feel the return of the brain tumor.

She says, "Look, I've been edgy lately. I need the cigarettes. How did the election go?"

"I won. Vicki won." I feel like a little kid bringing a drawing to my mother, not sure how she's going to react.

"Congratulations. Your father and I will take you all out for a dinner celebration." She pulls out another cigarette.

"I'm going to be press secretary," Andrew volunteers loudly.

My mother lights the second cigarette from the first. Chain smoking. I hate it.

The phone rings. Andrew answers it. "Bernie."

"Cassandra, we got you and your sister your own phone. Use it. Don't tie up mine."

I pick up the phone. "Hi, Bernie, do me a favor. Call me back on my phone. Give me a minute to get upstairs."

My room still looks as if a cyclone hit it. I clear a space on my bed and flop down just as the phone rings.

"Bernie?"

"Yes. Well?"

"I won."

"Fantastic. We'll have to celebrate."

"Vicki's going to have a party."

"Excellent." Bernie sounds happy. "As long as we don't spend the whole evening with the entire group."

We talk for a few minutes and then he says, "Listen, I've got to go. My sister wants to use the phone and is threatening me with immediate death if I don't get off this instant."

We hang up. Older sisters think they own any telephone in sight.

Stephie sticks her head in. "Cassie, can I speak to you, please."

"Sure, come in." I wonder what she wants from me.

She actually comes in, clears a space on my bed, and sits down.

"First of all, little sister, congratulations." She looks nervous. "I think it's wonderful that you won the election."

She must want something big. Come to think of it, she's left me alone for the last few days, and she was nice to me this morning.

She continues, "Look, I've got something to ask you."

I knew it.

She clears her throat. "This is difficult for me."

I stare at her. She's twirling her long blond hair around her finger.

"Yeah?" I ask. I don't want to make it too easy for her. Especially since she probably wants to use me.

"Well, you get along better with Mom than I do. Has she said anything to you lately about what's going on? Things are awful around here."

"You notice, too," I volunteer. "No, she hasn't said anything. What about Dad? He talks to you."

She looks at her long fingernails and starts biting one. "Not anymore. He's not here much, you know. Anyway, she always gets mad when I talk to him, so we don't talk anymore."

She looks upset. I can't believe it. She's still chewing her nail.

"Cassie," she continues, "I've been talking to Ms. Larson."

"My Ms. Larson?" I ask. "My art teacher?"

She nods. "She's my homeroom teacher, and one

day she noticed that I was really upset and asked if I wanted to talk. I got tired of keeping everything inside and pretending nothing bothers me, so I decided to trust her."

"My teacher. Did you tell her stories about what a lousy sister I am?"

"Cut it out," she says. "Look, she likes you a lot . . . said I should talk to you, that maybe we can learn not to compete."

"We don't compete," I say. "That's silly."

She makes a face. "Everything is always a contest in this house. Who's the prettiest? The best dressed? The smartest? The most popular? And you know who's the worst? *She* is. Our mother. She's the one who's got us all against each other. I hate her."

What an awful thing to say.

Stephie continues, "Ms. Larson thinks maybe we can help each other through all this. . . . Look, you just keep sitting there, not saying anything." Her voice gets louder. "Well, say something. If you don't want to work things out, then who cares?"

"No, I want to. It's just strange. We haven't talked since we were little."

"I blame her—our wonderful mother. Ms. Larson says I've got to be able to see Mother as a person, with her own problems. But I can't. I think Dad's a saint to put up with her, and that's what I want to talk about. I'm scared they're going to split up."

"Me too." I can't believe she feels the same way. "Stephie, what can we do?"

"About the marriage? Nothing, probably. I'm scared. If they get divorced, she'll get custody of us. And I know she hates me. She'll make it miserable for me. She's always telling me I'm not as pretty as I think I am . . . and Cassie, I don't think I'm that wonderful . . . really . . . I get scared just like everyone else. People always think if someone's pretty, she won't have any problems." She starts to cry. "I'm sick and tired of it. Sometimes I just wish I'd never been born."

She's never been like this before, at least not that I've ever seen. She looks absolutely terrible crying. Part of me likes the fact that she looks so bad. I never knew she felt this way. I reach out and pat her hair.

She hugs me and keeps crying. "Cassie, I'm so scared."

"Me too." I hold on to her, and then I start crying too. "And you're going away to college next year and leaving me all alone with it."

She starts sniffling. "But that's a long way away. You know, Ms. Larson said you didn't hate me. I didn't believe her."

"Do you hate me?" I ask, making a moustache out of my hair.

"No . . . you get on my nerves sometimes . . . getting all the attention of being sick, being the younger sister, getting better grades. But I would like us to get along, to be friends."

"Me too." I nod. I remember how we used to have fun when we were little.

"Sometimes I think I'll marry Greg just to get out of here, but then I'll be doing just what Mother did." She reaches for a Kleenex and blows her nose. If the prom queen committee could only see her now, I think.

"Look, Cassie," she continues, "Ms. Larson says we'll survive, but sometimes I really wonder."

I get out of bed, look in the jack-in-the-box I've had since I was four, and pull out the pistachios. "Want some?"

She nods.

"Whenever I get upset or feel sick, I eat these."

"So I noticed." She takes some. "You know what? Chocolate-covered graham crackers do the same thing for me."

"Mom keeps throwing my pistachios away," I say. "Sometimes I think there's only one way to manage it."

"How?"

I throw the shell into the garbage can. Two points. Stephie throws hers in. Tie score.

"Next time I go to the doctor, I'm going to ask for a pistachio prescription to cure all my problems."

"Think I can get one for chocolate-covered graham crackers?" Stephie laughs.

The phone rings. Stephie and I both go for it at the same time. I get it.

"It's Greg," I say.

She gets up and kisses me on the forehead. "I'll take it in my room. Cassie, I'm really glad we've talked. Let's keep doing this."

I nod and smile.

After she goes, I just sit there, not sure what I feel. What if I start trusting Stephie and she turns against me? What if my parents do split up? What if I'm not a good class president? Suppose Bernie decides he likes someone better than me?

The pistachio prescription—I wish it were real.

Chapter 11

There's a knock on my door. "Package for Ms. Cassandra Stephens. Pony Express."

Pony Express, ha. I know my father's voice when I hear it, although I hardly ever hear it anymore.

"Come in," I yell, "but only if your pony's house-trained."

He's grinning. "Cassie, congratulations, honey. I'm very proud of you."

He hugs me.

"Did Mommy tell you I won?" I ask, holding on to him.

"I called the school, asked for Mr. Zimmerman, and he told me. I've known for hours."

How embarrassing. I'll never be able to look Mr. Zimmerman in the eye again. He must think my family's crazy. But also, how wonderful—my father cares.

I take a good look at him. With all the time he spends away, traveling on business, I don't get much of a chance to look at him. He's still gorgeous—bright blue eyes, long eyelashes, nice and tall. Lots of girls at my school think he looks like a movie star. He certainly doesn't look forty.

"Mr. Zimmerman said he'd just announced it, so I was one of the first to know," my father says. "He also thinks you're a very nice person."

I stand there and grin.

"Cassie, it's treasure hunt time."

We used to do this when I was a kid.

"OK, Dad, give me a hint."

"Nope. Got to find it without a clue."

The old game—first I look behind his ear, then in it, and then in his mouth. When I was little I used to look more, but now that I'm older I get embarrassed. There's only one place it can be—in a jacket pocket.

I pulled out a present, beautifully gift-wrapped.

"Well, open it." He keeps smiling.

I don't want this ever to end.

"Cassie, don't just stand there, open it."

"Daddy, thank you."

"You don't even know what it is. How do you know you're going to like it?"

I shake it. "I just know." I pull off the wrapping and lift the lid.

It's a gold necklace that spells out "Love." It's just beautiful. I start to cry. "Oh, Daddy, I love it. I'll never take it off."

He helps me with the clasp. "Cassie, honey, no

matter what, I want you to remember how much I love you." He turns me around. "You know that, don't you?"

I nod.

"Tonight we're all going to celebrate your victory. I've made reservations at the country club for eight o'clock, so be downstairs by seven thirty." He gives me a kiss on the forehead and leaves.

I walk over to the mirror and stare at myself. The chain falls just right. I'm going to wear it until I'm a hundred years old. At least.

I look at my eyebrows. They're growing in a little stubby but not terrible. I decide to take the sunglasses off, to free my face.

By seven thirty, I've tried on every fancy outfit I own. I finally decide on my long peasant dress because it's got a halter top and my new necklace shows.

Everyone's waiting downstairs. Stephie looks beautiful. So does my mother. So does my father. And Andrew has all the catsup, jelly, and other junk wiped off him. I feel like going upstairs, starting all over again, but that's dumb. I can't be like this forever. So I act as if I belong. Maybe I really do. Maybe if I'm lucky the country club will have pistachio ice cream for dessert.

We all pile into the station wagon. Andrew sits between my parents, pretending to drive and going "Vroom, vroom" while my father gets ready to start the car.

Stephie says, "How about letting me drive?"

My father says, "Sure," just as my mother shakes her head and says, "No."

Stephie jumps out of the back seat and my father gets out of the front.

"Doesn't anyone listen to me anymore?" my mother says. "Don't I count at all?"

I shut my eyes and think, "Oh, no, please make them stop. Not today."

"Daddy said I could drive," Stephie says. "I've got to practice."

My father smiles nervously and says, "Come on, Anne, let's not argue tonight. I thought we decided to make it a pleasant evening."

My mother starts to cry. "I'm sick of pretending."

"Anne, I'm sick and tired of your amateur theatrics," he yells.

"Are you any better? Pretending everything's all right for tonight when we're going to tell them about the divorce next week. You're a hypocrite. You always were. You always will be."

Fighting on my special night.

A divorce.

Their divorce.

Our divorce.

"I can't stand it anymore," I yell. "Please stop." I get out of the car and run up to the porch. No door key. I can't get in. I won't go back to the car.

I can't breathe.

Feel like passing out.

I double over.

My father rushes over, picks me up, opens the door, carries me into the living room, and puts me on the couch. I try to tell him I can't breathe, but I can't even talk. My heart's beating in my eyes and forehead. I start coughing and try to get rid of the gunk collecting in my chest.

I can barely hear the voices. My mother's saying, "Cassie, darling, take your medicine. Don't punish yourself. I'm sorry it came out this way." She's still crying.

My father is saying, "We both love you very much. Please, Cassie."

"Cass, you've got to calm down, or we'll have to take you to the hospital. Please, honey."

I just lie there. The medicine's making me drowsy.

"I want to go up to my room," I say.

"Should I carry you?" my father asks.

"I don't need anything from either of you." So there, I think.

I get up. "I want to thank everyone for a lovely celebration," I say. "You can all go to hell."

Andrew starts crying.

"Not you. I still love *you*," I say and pat him on the arm as I leave. It's not easy walking up the steps. I feel exhausted. My eye keeps twitching. I'm crying and sniffling.

All my clothes are still on the bed. I push them onto the floor and lie down.

Stephie comes in. She's crying too.

I hug her and we cry together.

"Cassie, I'm sorry. I didn't mean for it to happen. Do you think this is all my fault?"

I just hug her.

Finally she says, "Cassie, I'm calling Greg and getting away from here for a while. Will you be OK?"

"What's OK? Breathing? Coming from a broken home? Yeah, I'll be OK, I guess. Have a good time."

"I just need to think everything out," she says.

As Stephie leaves, she asks, "Sure you're OK? I won't go if you're not."

I nod.

After she goes, I sit up and rock back and forth, thinking about setting fire to the house and trying to figure out whom I hate the most, my father or my mother.

My mother tiptoes in and sits down on the edge of my bed. "Cassie, it was inevitable. Your father and I have been talking about the divorce for a long time. We were going to tell you next week, but I think the strain was too much. I guess I just broke down tonight." She starts crying and picking up the clothes from the floor.

I try to turn off, not feel anything at all—not sorry or angry or anything. Just numb.

It doesn't work.

Sorry. I feel sorry for her. She's definitely not happy about what's happening. But I don't know what to do. How to help her. I'm having enough trouble helping myself. And I hate her. She's ruined my special evening.

She says, "I feel terrible about what happened. We'll talk everything out tomorrow." Then she kisses me on the cheek and leaves.

Talk everything out tomorrow. Garbage. What will that solve?

A knock on the door.

It's my father.

He walks over. "Cassie, I'm sorry it didn't work out. I guess your mother's right. There's no use pretending we can get along. It's over and that's all there is to it."

That's all.

As simple as that.

Three kids.

A broken-up family.

I look at him and take off my necklace. "Here, take this back. I don't want it."

There are tears rolling down his cheeks.

"Daddy, where are you going? What's going to happen? Are you going to marry someone else?" I stare at the necklace in my hand.

He says, "I'll take one of my apartments in the city. Your mother will have custody of all of you, but I'll have visitation rights. And there's nobody else in my life. Your mother and I aren't separating because of someone else. We just can't get along anymore."

Just can't get along. Damn. When Stephie and

Andrew and I fight, they're always telling us we've got to get along, that it's easy. Work it out, they say. So how come it's something for us to do and not them? Why aren't they working it out?

"I'm sorry, Cassie."

"If I promise to be real good and not have asthma attacks, will you stay?" I'm crying again.

Our whole family cries. We could probably fill up a dam.

He shakes his head. "You had nothing to do with it. I promise."

"When are you leaving?"

"Tomorrow. I think that's best."

I turn away from him.

"Cassie, I'm really sorry things have turned out this way." He gets up and slowly leaves.

I call Bernie, but his sister says he and his father have gone to see the Knicks play and won't be home until real late.

There's another knock on my door. If I can't see Bernie, I don't want to see anyone.

It's Andrew. "Cassie, can I sleep with you? I'm scared to be alone."

He's wearing his Snoopy pajamas and carrying his old baby blanket.

"Oh, OK," I say. "Just give me a chance to get changed."

I go into the bathroom to change, decide that it's not worth brushing my teeth, change, and go to bed. Andrew's already there asleep.

Well, Cassie, I say to myself, congratulations on being a winner.

Thank you, I answer.

Chapter 12_____

School's not canceled because my parents have split up. I've still got to preside over class meetings. Pounding the gavel to get order at the first meeting, I slammed it on my left hand. It took over a week for the swelling to go down. It looked gross, just gross. My eyebrows finally look normal, and then I have to end up with a hand that looks like King Kong's paw.

Mr. Meyerson has given three quizzes this week. I got a forty-two on the first one, a twenty-six on the second, and hit the big time with the third, an eleven.

Walking down the halls, I'm sure everyone can look at me and tell that my parents are getting a divorce. It's strange. When I used to hear about some kid's parents breaking up, I thought, big deal, it happens all the time. But now I know it's different. From now on, whenever I hear about a divorce, I'm going to know how bad the kid is really feeling.

I don't know what I'd do without Bernie. He's

been wonderful. I don't feel so all alone when I'm with him. And he's real good at holding me when I need it. Sometimes though, I get confused. There are times when I like being held and kissed. Then there are times when I think things are happening too fast; and other times, I wish things were happening faster. I wish I understood more about sex, but I don't and I don't think Bernie does either. Maybe I should talk to Stephie or Vicki, but it's so embarrassing being an amateur. And talking about real personal stuff isn't easy. I'm afraid they'll think I'm a silly little kid who's making a big deal out of nothing.

I'm always smiling at school. I'll probably win an academy award for my stunning performance, unless it goes to Stephie. But whoever wins, the other will get the award for supporting actress. My sister always acts as if everything's just wonderful. She's still nice to me, but she makes sure that she doesn't stay around the house much at all. And she acts depressed and angry when she's home.

To top it all off, I've got to go see Mr. Zimmerman to talk about the Freshperson Class Day.

One day a year, each class is allowed to pick out a special activity for the whole school to participate in. The senior class is planning a combination picnic and teach-in on pollution. The junior class is planning a role-playing day, when everybody in the entire school is to come in as a historical person. Each teacher will be responsible for planning an activity in which we have to write or speak as that historical person. The sophomore class still doesn't know what it's doing.

There are times when I hate being class president. This is one of them. The only time I've ever hated it more was when I realized I need to know math to be a good president—to figure out majority percentages, to check treasurer's reports. Now I've got to tell Mr. Zimmerman that we want an "Awareness of Physical Fitness Day," on which all the classes will deal with segments of its history, nutrition, controversies, and anything else we can think of. That part's fine, wonderful in fact. That's the good news. The bad news is that the majority of the kids (two thirds) voted that we should show our physical fitness by spending the entire day on roller skates. It's a dumb idea, funny, but dumb. I just know Mr. Zimmerman's going to kill me when I tell him. He's been good so far, but even I think this is going too far.

His secretary comes up to me. "Cassie, Mr. Zimmerman will see you now."

I smile at her and try to look presidential.

Mr. Zimmerman is standing behind his desk. "Hi, Cassie, sit down."

As I plop myself into the chair, I think I should probably try to look more official. It's hard to be thirteen and look official in the principal's office.

He's smiling. "I understand this meeting is about the Freshman Class Day."

Freshperson, I think.

He's still smiling.

I nod. "We want to have an 'Awareness of Physical Fitness Day.'"

"Wonderful."

"And we want everyone to spend the entire day on roller skates."

"Not so wonderful." He's still got a smile on his face, but I can tell he's not going to OK the suggestion.

"It's what the class voted on."

"Cassie, what do you think of this idea?"

No fair, he's asking me to be a fink, to tell him that the class has done something silly. I can't be a traitor. They voted for me.

"The class majority voted for it," I say.

"I didn't ask you that. I asked what you think of it."

I shrug. "It could be fun."

"It's too dangerous. What about going up and down the steps on roller skates? Can you imagine the risk? And what about the students and teachers who are handicapped or don't know how to skate?"

"I guess I'll have to go back to them and tell them no, that we've got to start all over."

"And make me the bad guy?"

I nod and say, "Sure, better you than me."

"Cassandra, do you think that that's the best way to handle the situation? Do you think there's a better way? I think the first part of the idea is excellent. Physical fitness is essential to the whole person. I could use more knowledge about it. I just don't want the roller skates. And if being dangerous were not enough reason to veto it, can you imagine what our floors would look like?"

I sit there quietly and feel like squirming.

He continues, "Now, I'm sure that it would be pretty funny seeing some of us on roller skates. I bet you can think of several people you'd like to see, shall we say, not on their feet. But do you understand my reasoning?"

"Yes, I do."

"Don't you think the rest of the class will understand it?"

I nod and think about how Bobby Franklin wanted everyone on roller skates also to wear blindfolds. But then I think how some kids offered an alternate possibility for when Mr. Zimmerman vetoed this one. Somehow I think we all knew what he was going to say.

"Well, why don't you go back to them and discuss it further."

"OK."

He gets up and says, "It was nice speaking to you. Feel free to make an appointment any time. I think you're doing a fine job. Be sure to say hello to your father for me. He seems like a very nice man."

I feel like saying, "Just because he called you to find out if I won doesn't make him wonderful. He's a family deserter." But I don't. It would be mortifying. So I just nod and smile instead.

On the way to class, I think about my father and how much I miss him. It's strange. We spend one day each weekend with him, the three of us. That's more time than we got when he lived with us. But it's not good. He plans one activity for the three of us, and it never works out.

The week we went to the Metropolitan Museum of Art, I loved it. But Andrew and Stephie just kept rushing by all the paintings I wanted to look at more closely. It was a mess. I ended up at the special exhibit; Andrew in the armor room; Stephie at the costume exhibit; my father at the restaurant. So we spent our time together separately.

The week we went to the Museum of Natural History, Andrew stayed in the room with the whale; I went to the folk dance exhibit; Stephie to rocks and minerals; my father to the snack bar.

We all went to the same Broadway play, too, even sat through it together. But who's got a chance to talk during a play? Afterward we went to dinner. Andrew ate one of my father's order of *escargots*—that's snails—and threw up on the table.

Getting a divorce is a real drag on the kids. We have less time for our friends, more planned activities; both parents aren't there when you want them; and sometimes we've got to deal with more moods from the parents.

Mother's getting the house, the station wagon, alimony, child support, the credit cards, and us. She got into a fight with Stephie the other day because Steph said she was "making out like a bandit." My mother hit the ceiling, said Dad was getting off cheap. She'd given up a lot trying to please him. She was the one left with the responsibility of raising us, and if Stephie hates her that much, she should go live with her father. It was an awful scene. Stephie called up Dad right after that. When she came back out of her room, she didn't say anything. Just looked as if she'd been crying.

I'm at the door to Ms. Larson's classroom. Taking a deep breath before I go in, I try to look as if I'm in total control. She knows all about everything. After I found out that Stephie had talked to her, I was sort of shy, but she came over and told me not to worry. Sometimes I want to talk to her, but I sort of think she's Stephie's friend, so I don't say anything. But I know she'd understand. I just don't want the kids to know I'm not in total control, really not much in control at all.

I walk in and sit down at a table with Bernie. Having someone who saves me a seat makes me feel much better.

Ms. Larson is lecturing about quilts. "So you see, since many people were poor, they used every scrap of material they had. It's not like today, when people waste so much."

I think of all the clothes in my mother's closet. And all the new stuff she's buying now that she is, as she says, "into the dating scene."

It's gross. My own mother acting like a kid, talking on the phone to her friends about different guys. It's a nightmare. When she goes out at night, sometimes she doesn't come in until real late. I lie in bed listening for her to return.

Ms. Larson's still talking. "The quilts that were made had scraps from everything that could be used—old clothes, blankets, curtains, anything else that could no longer be used in its original shape. The patterns came out of experiences and needs. Quilts for births, for weddings, special occasions, so that the time spent making them was a celebration of a celebration."

I wonder if they make quilts for divorces. After it's all finished, they can cut it in half so that each person ends up with something.

"It was a way for women to be creative, to make patterns that were unique." She holds up some pictures and starts passing them around. "Some of the patterns have become traditional, like the log cabin, the wedding ring."

I wonder what kinds of traditions divorced families have. It makes me sad. And jealous—jealous of everyone who has a whole family.

"I want everyone to bring in some material, including at least one piece that's got real importance for you." She smiles. "And then we're going to make a class quilt. It'll be a good way for you to gain appreciation for the art form. I also want you to figure out how many squares will be necessary to make a full-size quilt."

Math again. I feel betrayed. Math in an art class. It's unfair.

Sara Baskin asks, "What are we going to do with the finished quilt?"

Ms. Larson says, "Put it up on exhibit for a while. Then I'm not sure. Any suggestions?"

Bernie raises his hand.

"Bernard, let's hear this one." Ms. Larson looks as if she's not sure what to expect, but figures it's going to be off the wall.

"We should coordinate this with what we learn in other classes. Right? That way the Board of Education will know we're getting a well-rounded learning experience, becoming Renaissance people. Right?"

"Get to the point, Bernie," she says.

He grins. "In history class, we learned that during colonial times, they had a custom called bundling. I think the entire class should recreate that custom."

"The Board of Education would just love hearing about an entire class and one quilt. I've grown very fond of this job. 'Fraid not. Any other suggestions?"

Brenda Curtis raises her hand. "I think we should raffle it off and donate the proceeds to that fund set up to try to preserve Appalachian folk arts."

Beaming, Ms. Larson says, "Excellent."

I write Bernie a note. "Now *that* is a good idea. *Some* people (I won't mention any names) are trying to get reputations as weirdos."

He reads it and writes back, "I already have a

reputation as a weirdo. I'm trying to get one as a sex maniac."

I answer, "And what will that do to *my* reputation?"

He does his Groucho imitation.

Ms. Larson says, "Do any of you have any idea of what you're going to bring in?"

"My old rugby shirt," Jack Bradley yells.

"One of my grandmother's very old handkerchiefs," Sandy Cole offers.

"My cutoffs from junior high."

"I'll bring in something my daughter's outgrown," Ms. Larson says.

I never think of her as a mother. I'm jealous of her kid.

"One of my father's ugly ties," says Cynthia Wharton.

I decide: part of my old baby blanket.

When the bell rings, I'm still thinking about my family breaking up.

Bernie and I walk down the hall.

"Would a penny for your thoughts be enough? Or has inflation caused it to go up?" he asks.

"These aren't even worth a plugged nickel. It's just the divorce thing again. I just wish everything was the way is used to be."

He takes my hand. "But the way it was wasn't good. That's why they split up. I keep telling you that."

"Yeah, but I keep thinking that if they only tried once more it would work out this time."

He shrugs. "I've given up on my family. I'm just trying to deal with them without hassles."

I don't understand it. If all anybody wants is to be happy, then how come things don't work out?

"Come on, Bernie," I sigh, "we're going to be late."

I really get sick of it. Always having to be in a chair at a certain time, to do what someone else wants me to do.

We rush. Terry Chamberlain comes up, stops me, and says, "Cassie, I want to talk to you about the way our class always gets last choice at the electives. It's your duty as class president to—"

I interrupt. "Look, Terry, we'll talk later. I'm running late."

"Getting a swelled head now, too big for your own britches. I should have figured your campaign promises meant nothing. The people's candidate. *Bull!*" He turns and leaves.

I call after him, but he rounds a corner.

Bernie says, "Talk to him later. We're real late."

We run to class.

Detention for running and for being late.

Stoddard got us. He's such a worm.

Sometimes it's a dictatorship.

These are supposed to be the best years of my life. I wish they'd come with satisfaction guaranteed or double my money back.

Chapter 13

Andrew, Stephie, and I have decided to hold a family conference, junior members only.

We meet in the tree house.

Stephie pulls the twigs out of her hair. "Couldn't we have met in the house?"

"More private here," I say.

Andrew plays host and passes around Kool-Aid and Oreos.

We all sit quietly for a few minutes.

I watch how each of us eats the cookies.

Andrew takes the top off and eats it first. Then he licks off the creme, eating the bottom last.

Stephie takes small bites of the whole cookie.

I eat the top off the cookie, push all the creme into one corner of the bottom layer, and eat it until I reach the end. Then I put the creme on my finger while I eat the rest of the wafer. I eat the creme filling last.

Somehow I think there's a lesson to be learned

from my observation of cookie eaters, but I'm not sure what it is.

Andrew says, "I think we should try to get Mommy and Daddy back together."

"I'd rather try to figure out a way to get her out of this house and Daddy back in," Stephie says.

"Not practical," I say.

"I can dream, can't I?"

"We've got to do this fast before either of them finds someone else to marry," I say. "Also before the divorce becomes final."

"They could remarry if that happens," Stephie says. "We could be bridesmaids at our own parents' wedding." She makes a terrible face. "How gross!"

Andrew says, "I want Daddy home so he can play ball with me again. He doesn't have time to do that anymore now that the three of us go out together."

"A package deal, that's what we are," Stephie says.

I make a mental note to ask Bernie if he wants to join Andrew and me to play baseball sometime. Stephie takes out polish for her nails. "I really don't think this is going to work. I'm not even sure it should work. Those two are definitely not a matched pair."

"But I want us to be a whole family," I say.

"Me too, but I don't think we should get our hopes up."

"Look, if you don't want to help, that's fine. Just let us know."

"It's not that I won't help," says Stephie. "I just don't think it's going to do any good."

Andrew says, "Let's start."

"We need suggestions of ways to bring them back together," Stephie says.

"We can tell them that we're becoming socially maladjusted and warped as a result of the break-up," I suggest.

Stephie giggles. "They'll just say that we were already socially maladjusted and warped before the breakup."

"Well, we can all get some weird disease that can only be cured through constant close care by both parents."

"It'll never work," Andrew says. "They'll take us to Dr. O'Malley, and he'll tell them we're faking."

Stephie looks up from her nails. "Why don't we just talk to each of them separately and tell them how we feel?"

"Good idea," I say.

She points. "*You* talk to Mom. *I'll* talk to Dad."

"Who do I talk to, the avocado plant?" Andrew asks.

Stephie and I exchange glances.

"Which one do you want to talk to?" I ask.

"Both. Let me go to both," he begs.

A deal. They both adore him. Maybe it will work.

We plan all the strategies: who cries when; how to look assertive yet pitiful; how to calm each one down initially; how to explain that staying together will be less expensive; how to let them know how much happier the kids will be.

After we finish, Andrew refills the glasses with Kool-Aid and passes out more Oreos.

Stephie says, "No thanks, got to watch my weight."

I, as the teenage totem, don't have to, but decide not to have any more anyway—due to a recurring nightmare that one day the dentist is going to inform me that all my teeth have rotted, that I'd better organize a telethon to pay for the work on my mouth.

Andrew asks, "Do you think this is going to work?"

I immediately say, "Yeah."

Stephie immediately says, "No."

"Yes," Andrew says. "I break the tie."

Stephie sighs. "It's not going to be that easy. Mom and Dad have the only votes that count in this thing. I don't want to see us hurt any more than we already are. We may just have to get used to the situation. Greg lives with just one parent. He manages."

"But that's different. His father died. He didn't get a divorce," I say.

"I'm just saying things could be worse. We still have a father. Greg doesn't. He's had lots of feelings to work out because of his father's heart attack. He feels deserted, sad, guilty, angry—just the way we do—but at least we still have a father to talk to."

We all sit quietly.

I'd never realized that Greg felt so strongly, hurt so much. He always seems so secure.

The older I get, the more I learn about people. Sometimes I wish there wasn't so much to learn and that I didn't have to find out about it.

"Well, we should try," Andrew says. "John's mother and father are together again."

True. They worked it out. I once overheard Ms. Brandon and my mother talking about how John started wetting his bed when his parents split up. Maybe if the three of us started wetting our beds, they'd take the hint. If it worked out for John, why not for us?

Stephie says, "I've got to go now. Margie's having a review session for our trig test."

Trigonometry. I can't even do algebra yet. I should forget about college prep. Maybe by the time I'm a senior they'll have invented a pill that unblocks the part of the brain that deals with math.

We work our way out of the tree house. I almost trip on a loose board. Just what I'd need. A ten-foot fall.

Mother's in the kitchen preparing dinner when we walk in.

"Listen," she says, "I want the three of you to help out around the house more. I spend entirely too much time in the kitchen."

"You get paid well enough for it," Stephie mutters.

Mother turns to Stephie, looking as if she's going

to throw a scoop of mashed potatoes at her. "What did you say?"

"Nothing. Skip it." Stephie turns and walks out.

"Well, I'm serious about this," Mother says to Stephie's back.

"What do you want us to do?" Andrew asks.

Mother sits down. "More chores. A little more of the cooking. I've been thinking about how much of my life's been spent being a maid, cook, housekeeper. I want more time for myself."

Wonderful. Maybe if the divorce happens, she'll leave too. Neither of them will get custody of us.

I wonder how Bernie would feel about marrying me, if his father would go on paying orthodontist bills. We could adopt Andrew and take the dowry. If we got married, we could always sit together in classes where seating is alphabetical.

Marriage to Bernie. Bad idea. By the time I'm twenty-six, I will have been married half my life.

Mother continues, "I've got a date tonight, so I want you children to do the dinner dishes."

"Who are you seeing?" I ask, not sure I really want to know.

She smiles. "A business associate of Mrs. Fulton's. I met him at a dinner party at her house. He's very nice. I'm sure you'll like him."

Like him. I don't even want him to darken our doorstep. I change the subject. "Andrew and I want to talk to you about something."

"What?"

"Maybe some other time. I'm not sure it's good timing right now," I say.

"No, tell me."

"We want you and Daddy to stay married," Andrew says.

She turns to the counter. "No, I refuse to talk about it, not after the way that man's treated me."

I start to do all the things we talked about in the tree house, but she stamps her foot.

"I will not hear of this. Leave me alone. I'm sorry you're unhappy, but live with it. I've got to."

"Please," Andrew says.

"No more talking now," she says. "Look, I've got to get ready for my date. Milt's going to be here in about an hour. So let's just drop it."

She goes upstairs.

Andrew and I end up eating dinner alone.

"Maybe after we talk to Daddy and he apologizes it'll work out," he says.

I nod but realize that Stephie is probably right.

Milton arrives. Mom's big date. I answer the door and hate him instantly. He's wearing a shirt that's unbuttoned to the middle of his chest, gold chains around his neck. He tells me that I'm "a cute kid."

She comes down the steps, wearing a tan jump suit, a designer scarf, and boots. A basic, everyday suburban mother.

As they leave, Andrew's saying stuff like, "Don't stay out too late" and "If you drink, don't drive."

I debate calling out, "Don't do anything I wouldn't do," which definitely wouldn't leave her with much, but I decide she might kill me.

Once they're gone, Andrew turns to me and says, "Dad's better."

I nod and try to imagine what it would be like to have that creep as a stepfather.

I can feel the return of my headache—Brain Tumor, Part II.

Chapter 14

Two strikes and we were out. Dad won't come home.

What did work out was a change in the visiting schedule. One Sunday a month, all three of us go into the city to see Dad. Then he takes each of us separately one Sunday a month. That means less time to see him, but more time to be alone with him.

Andrew's up in his tree house. Stephie's over at Greg's. Mom's still in bed asleep. Last night she had a date with a new guy, Arnold the Accountant. A real drip.

The freshperson class is having a combination bake sale and car wash tomorrow to raise money for our class project. We've decided to contribute to a rehabilitation center for handicapped kids. We're going to use the money for books for their library. Then a group of us will go to the center to work with the kids. I like this idea a lot better than the "Roller Skate Caper."

Vicki, Bernie, and Peter Leonardi are coming

over to make cookies and brownies for tomorrow. Peter and Vicki started going out right after she got a letter from Kris, saying that from California to New Jersey was too far and he was dating a cheerleader.

Vicki arrives first. "Hear about Stoddard?"

I shake my head.

"He's applied for the vice-principal's job for next year, after Mr. Rogers resigns."

Just what I need, that rat in a position of real power. He gets worse, not better.

Vicki continues, "I hope they hire a woman."

I wouldn't care if they hired a hamster. As long as it's not Stoddard.

Peter arrives next. "Sorry I'm late, my father made me mow the lawn first." He's still holding on to his ten-speed bike as he comes in the front door.

"Want to park that in the garage," I say.

He nods. "Ever since the last one got stolen, I'm real careful."

Bikes get stolen around here all the time. It's awful. I think there's a gang of juvenile delinquents in this town who are trying to work their way into a major crime syndicate when they grow up. They must get points for every bike they turn in.

Bernie arrives next. He's carrying a dandelion, which he presents to me.

I thank him, curtsy, and we all head into the kitchen.

After we make the first batch of cookies, Bernie asks, "Where's Andrew? We should let him have some of these."

"In the tree house," I say, licking the spoon.

He heads out to find Andrew.

Bernie's back fast, out of breath. "Andrew's hurt. He fell out of the tree. I just found him."

We all rush out.

Andrew's lying there trying to smile. Another tooth's gone; his right leg's folded under him. There's blood on his head and he looks dazed.

"Andrew, are you OK?" I ask.

He says, "It hurts," and starts to cry.

"Bernie, Peter, stay with him," I order. "I'll get Mom. Vicki, call an ambulance."

I rush upstairs, yelling, "Mom!"

She comes out of the bedroom, pulling on a sweatshirt. She's in blue jeans. "Cassie, what is it?"

"Andrew's hurt. Fell out of the tree house. Come quick."

She rushes downstairs. I've never seen her move so fast. I follow.

When she gets to him, he says, "Mommy, it hurts."

She reaches out, touches his head where it's bleeding, and says, "I'm sure it does. You'll be all right though. Don't worry."

She's very pale, but also very calm.

"Ms. Stephens," Vicki says, "the ambulance is on the way."

"Thanks."

My mother motions me over to the side. "Cass, call your father. He'll want to know."

I nod and rush inside. Vicki comes with me.

"Oh, Vicki," I say, "this is all my fault. I knew there was a loose board there. I didn't do anything about it. If Andrew comes out of this OK, I'll do anything . . . I'll even give up pistachio nuts."

I reach the phone and dial the number. A woman answers. I can't stand it. What right does she have to be in his apartment in the morning?

"Is Andrew Stephens, Sr., there?" I yell.

"Who shall I say is calling?" she asks.

"His daughter, damn it! Tell him it's an emergency."

"Just a minute," she says.

I can hear the ambulance siren.

My father gets on the phone. "Stephie? Cassie? What's going on?"

"It's Andrew. He fell out of the tree house. Mom said to call you."

"Where is she? Let me talk to her."

"She's out there with him. The ambulance is coming."

He says, "Tell them I'm on my way. I'll meet you at the hospital as soon as possible."

"OK."

I hang up. I wonder if he'll bring *her* back.

Vicki and I run back outside. They're loading Andrew onto the stretcher.

"Dad'll meet you at the hospital," I say.

"They want us to follow in the car," my mother says. "Let's go."

"We'll finish up here," Vicki offers.

I rush to the car. "And tell Stephie if she comes in or calls."

Bernie yells, "Call us and let us know what's happening."

"OK," I yell out the window.

By the time we get to the hospital emergency room, they've already taken him up for X rays. My mother's got to answer eighty zillion questions. It's a good thing we've got insurance.

The nurse comes out and says, "He's going to be all right. His leg's broken, and he's got a concussion. But he's going to be all right."

It could have been so much worse. I'm glad it's not. I start to cry. So does my mother.

My father rushes in. He's alone. My mother tells him the results.

"Why weren't you watching him?" he asks her.

She looks startled.

He continues, "Well, I want an explanation. How did this happen?"

"He fell out of the tree house, the one you built for him, the one I told you was too dangerous for a seven year old," my mother yells.

Everyone's looking at them. I tug on their arms. "Please, don't do this."

There's silence for a few moments. Then my

mother says, "Four days out of a month don't balance against what I've got to do. Don't you ever put it all on me."

I'm glad she said that.

"I'm sorry. I just got upset. I apologize."

"Accepted," my mother says with a frown.

The doctor comes in. "You may go up and see him now. He's OK, but we have to keep him in for observation. Concussion. Six stitches in his head. A clean break in his right leg. He'll recover."

We thank him and head for the elevator. On the way, we stop off and pick up comics, crayons, and coloring books at the gift shop.

We're all very quiet on the way up. We get off on Andrew's floor. The place smells sort of like a combination of Vicks VapoRub and lemons.

Andrew's lying in bed. There's a white bandage on his head. Plaster on his leg. Very pale.

He tries to sit up and yells, "Mommy! Daddy!" My mother makes him lie down again.

"Guess what?" he says. There's a bigger gap in his mouth where there used to be a tooth and a half more.

"What?" I ask.

"I swallowed a tooth. Guess where the doctor says it's going to come out?"

My father says, "Andrew, don't you dare try to get it back. The tooth fairy will leave you the money anyway. I'll write a note explaining the situation, and you can leave it under your pillow. That'll work."

I want to laugh.

My mother says, "Can we get you anything?" She's stroking his head.

Andrew motions over to his roommate. "That's Danny. He's had his knee operated on, like the football players do."

We all say hello to Danny. He looks like a terror. I bet the nurses are going to go nuts with both these kids.

"Danny and I want pizza."

I do laugh. What an operator.

My mother looks at my father, smiles at Andrew, and then says, "We'll see if it's allowed. If it is, we'll get you one."

My parents leave the room.

"Maybe now they'll get together," Andrew says.

I gasp. "Did you do this intentionally?"

"No, but as long as it's happened, maybe they'll get to talk and like each other again. I didn't try to do this. It was the loose board. I forgot."

I want to tell him the truth, that it'll never work out, that it'll never be the way it was or the way we want it to be. That we're going to have to accept things the way they are now. That we'll survive.

But he's only seven. So I don't say anything.

"Cassie, will you feed all my pets while I'm gone?"

I nod.

"And walk Snurful?"

Smiling, I remember what's happened the other

times I've had to take out that monster. He walks me. "Sure, Andrew."

"And Cassie?"

"Yes?"

"Will you decorate my cast all special?"

"Sure," I say, wondering what kind of paint to use on plaster.

While he talks to Danny about pizza, I sit there, holding his hand and thinking how much I want pistachios.

Then I remember my promise.

No more pistachios.

Never.

Not ever.

Oh, well, they didn't work anyway.

Twinkies, I bet, are the answer.

A NOTE FROM PAULA

When my first book, THE CAT ATE MY GYMSUIT, was published . . . I was soooo proud, soooo surprised. I was actually a WRITER . . . AND the book was doing well.

Then I showed three pages of my new book (all that I had written) to my editor and he said, "Okay. We'll buy it." The contracts were signed. I got some advance money . . . . and then the trouble started. I COULDN'T WRITE THE BOOK.

No one told me about "Second Book Block." The symptoms are the inability to write and worrying about whether you have anything more to say and whether you've "fooled" everyone into thinking that you can write.

It took three years to write that second book, THE PISTACHIO PRESCRIPTION.

Once after a speech, someone told me that it was her favorite book when she was growing up. She was now getting an autographed book for her daughter, Cassie. I said, "What a coincidence. She has the same name as the character in the book." The woman told me that it was no coincidence....that she had named her after the character.

That's one of the most special moments for me as a writer.

It means a lot to me, especially since the book was so hard for me to write, that so many people love and identify with it.

—Paula Danziger